A Life Stage Soundcheck

RACHEL VEZNAIAN

ISBN: 978-0-9990149-9-8

CONTENTS

I DON'T WANNA GROW UP

"What do you mean I'm running out of time?"
"Ran."
"What?"
"You ran out of time, Mr. Fredericks. Sorry to mince words. You ran out of time."
"But I… had no warning! No notice! How could you do this to me?"
"Actually, the multiple late notices you received indicate that you were warned well in advance. I'm not doing anything to you, just schlepping into work every day like everyone else."
"Ugh, sorry. You're right, but look. I couldn't pay that bill. I just couldn't." The frantic male voice emitting from Carla Cafaro's receiver continued grasping for justification.
"Well sir, the way you budget money is only of consequence to you." Carla said, remaining firm.
"But it's not just me. I have responsibili–"

"You mean like the responsibility of paying off your credit cards?"

"I don't just have to take care of me, okay?"

"I don't see any dependents listed here," Carla murmured in confusion, checking her notes.

"No. It's… it's not *that,*" Mr. Fredericks returned, his defensiveness falling away entirely. "It's my cat!" It was the falsetto he applied to the word *cat* that broke through her resolve. It was so pitiful.

"Your cat," she repeated, trying to deadpan.

"Yeah, man," he had begun to sob into the phone—the ugly cry of auditory communication Carla knew all too well. "She had all these complications. Her kidneys blew out and she went blind. Next thing you know, she falls down the stairs. Broken leg. Just like that. Have you heard of kitty wheelchairs?"

"No? I mean no. No, I have not. I assume they're costly."

"So, so much."

"Well, I'm sorry to hear that," Carla said, instantly regretting it. *Shit.* She should not be sympathizing with him.

"No you aren't—I can hear it in your voice! You don't care about Guccibear, and why would you?"

She at least still had him in the phone. He must have been lonely, and clearly lacked experience with debt collectors. They never lasted this long. "Have you ever considered relocating Gu… Guccibear, was it? Maybe to live with a relative?" She knew engaging further was taking her down a dangerous road.

"Of course not! What kind of monster are you?"

Carla tried to pivot, though her heart wasn't in it. "Hey, buddy. Cats live twenty years, but bad credit is forever."

"Fuck you!"

The receiver clicked, the man's voice vanishing into a dial tone. "I'll talk to you tomorrow," she said to no one. Carla plopped her receiver down. It wasn't exactly a shock. Carla's initial gusto with which she had accepted the position had faded over the last six years and with it her success at nailing down her skips. Now, Guccibear and Guccibear's dad were just the latest examples in a recent string of failures.

On the upside, the day was over and since her boss, Arthur, wasn't in on Fridays during the summer, she wouldn't have to go full stealth mode and sneak out. She could hold her head high as she marched with her comrades, an army of pasty, doughy, polyester suit-wearing coworkers.

Outside, muggy July air greeted her and treated her hair in the way a stylist with an eggbeater might. She tried to shove her unruly dark curls into a bun, but they had other plans, haphazardly popping out all over the place. Headphones were her next priority and, as she fit the cups snuggly over her ears, Grouplove ignited her and stimulated her brain. Though the humidity pierced the woven plastic pants and seemingly refused to leave, a veritable Hotel California of work wear, she tolerated the swamp that had formed in her trousers and chose to walk home from Downtown Boston rather than brave a sardine-like T car. She made her way through the Common and down Charles Street, passing the stressed masses heading home from work and the carefree jubilation of college students on break. Her gaze settling on the students, she thought absentmindedly, *I'll be chatting with all of you in a few years.*

Once she made her way beyond the midpoint of the Longfellow Bridge and pierced the tech barrier, suits magically became t-shirts, and briefcases turned into backpacks. She was getting closer to home. Only a couple miles now.

It occurred to her that she was awfully hot, and Summer's bookstore was awfully close by. Rather than torture herself by sitting in a non-air-conditioned studio apartment, maybe she could just pester her best friend for a minute or two.

"Hey good lookin, whatcha got cookin?" the upbeat sound of Summer's voice cut through "Welcome to Your Life" and Carla's train of thought.

"Oh, you know, same old same old. I finished my day by having a back and forth with some guy about his cat." Carla said as she entered the bookstore, rushing to close the door and keep the heat at bay.

"What guy?"

"A guy I was chasing after for money," Carla said. She walked to the back where Summer sat behind a cash register.

"And he told you about his cat?"

"Yeah, the poor thing's kidneys blew out."

"I can definitely tell you that my day wasn't even half that interesting." Summer twisted a string of jet-black hair around her finger and sighed, her gaze rolling around her parents' bookstore.

"Slow?"

"Might as well be stopped. We need something new to draw people in here."

"Today, I learned that the cat needed a kitty wheelchair. I feel like cats in kitty wheelchairs would attract people."

"Umm…. no." Summer said flatly. "I was thinking more along the lines of like a coffee shop. Look!"

Summer brightened as she indicated a set of bookcases that were particularly dusty up at the front end, flouncing over to them. "No one even *likes* the Romantic period, right? We can just shove these somewhere else and put in a couple of those cute little round tables. I already make coffee anyway, so just add in some pastries too and there you go!"

"What about lattes and stuff?"

"Whatd'ya mean?"

"Well, foofy people who hang out in coffee shops banging away on their keyboards at that novel they'll never publish always want a cappuccino or a macchiato or something."

"What's even the difference?"

Carla shrugged, "Beats me."

Summer's mouth twisted around in a contemplative moment. "Well, maybe if people stick around for my coffee and all the pastries I buy in bulk from Costco, then I can get an espresso machine."

"Sounds like a plan to me."

"And *then*…" Summer began. Carla braced herself, knowing how a drawn out *then* always signaled one of Summer's wistful tangents. "…maybe some live entertainment can come on in!"

Summer waggled her eyebrows, but Carla wasn't in the mood to play. "Oh so like Jas?"

"No, you fool, like *you*!"

"Doesn't sound like the people who come here to drink crappy coffee and read your books for free are gonna like hearing me bang away on my guitar to the top forty from the seventies."

"I mean, there's always the option to do something a little more current…"

"The Red Hot Chili Peppers aren't nearly as satisfying on acoustic."

"I was thinking like *now*."

"What? You want, like, Kygo or something? I mean, I guess? Sure?"

"No! *You*, you moron. Just play your own stuff."

"I don't have my own stuff."

"Liar."

"No. No, no, no, no. I have my feet firmly planted in the seventies, eighties, and nineties."

Summer walked back to the register once more

with a sigh, "You have your feet planted firmly in the guitar version of karaoke."

"Oh, hey now," Carla followed Summer back to her perch. "There's a difference between karaoke and covers."

"Covers at open mic nights aren't gonna pay the bills."

"Neither are originals at open mic nights."

"Have it your way. Collect debt for the rest of your life."

"Well, see, now once upon a time I was good at it."

"Mhmm, but now it's looking like you're just a therapist for your skips."

"True, true, I s'pose I could've first finished at Berklee, built up some student loans and then spent the rest of my life with a degree in music… while I chased skips."

Summer rolled her big brown eyes yet again, waving away their circular conversation. "Anyway, speaking of open mic nights, you wanna head down to Purple Salmon?"

"Yeah, I haven't heard anyone murder Journey in at least a couple nights."

"Watch the store for a minute while I close up the back," Summer said, sliding from her stool.

"Oh, I don't know, I may not be able to hold off the hoards trying to get through the front."

"Ha, ha."

Carla took up her own place on the stool, leaning into the counter and balancing her head on her hands. Her job was boring beyond belief, but it had to be better than this. She looked around at the completely dead space. The only sign of life came from the speakers Summer was beaming music into from her phone.

It was this rhythmic rolling of calypso sounds that mingled with harmonized *la la las* which always sent Carla backward in time.

She was six and wobbling around outside to "Sweat," which her sister had tuned their boom box to. That summer was a hot one and Carla was perpetually bored; Josie had attained a level of cool that most ten-year-olds on the precipice of middle school aspired to, so playing with her little sister was no longer an option.

Carla watched her lay there in a fold-back lawn chair on the cracked pavement in their back yard, which her mother, in vain, had painted green, an attempt to recreate the foliage that existed on lawns in the far-out suburbs. Josie was trying once again to tan, also an exercise in futility as there weren't nearly enough patches of sun large enough for such a venture. The shadows from the houses all around continued to creep into the line of UV and she would inevitably have to move once again.

Carla had made a feeble attempt at trying to get Josie to chase her around with the hose, a fruitless venture, and while she was perfectly comfortable with jumping in and out of the puddles she made on her own, it really just didn't have the same effect as when you were with someone else. On one particularly amusing occasion, Carla had come up with the brilliant plan to simply spray Josie. Surely the reason Josie wouldn't play with her was because she wasn't in the mood to get wet. The obvious answer there was to just foist wetness upon her and the problem would be instantly solved. A wet Josie would have to play with her. She was already wet! As it turned out, Josie didn't have to play with her at all. In fact, Josie then screamed at her and called for their mother as she ran back inside, leaving Carla to her own devices.

That particular day, as she wobbled and bounced to the sweet sounds of this man who, for some reason, wanted to make *you* sweat, she tried a different tactic.

"JOSIE?!"

Josie, wearing a day-glow one piece, as their mother still wouldn't allow her a bikini, lifted her head up in irritation, "You don't have to yell, Carla. What?"

"Wi- wi- will you play with me?"

Josie's head plunked down again, "No, Carla. I'm working on my tan."

"But it's summer!"

"I don't want to. Can't you just splash in the puddles or something?"

"But it isn't as much fun alone… Wanna spray me with the hose?"

"No. Buzz off."

Carla sighed and picked up the hose, letting the cool water rain down over before repositioning the spout at her mouth for a long drink. She spit out the excess water, trying to sing at the same time. She coughed and giggled, unable to keep up with the rhythm.

"*La glog la glog gla gla gla la…*"

"Shush, Carla! God."

First she had to play by herself and now Josie wouldn't even let her sing? Carla drummed her fingers along the hose, giggling as a plan formed in her mind. "Okay," she giggled.

"*What?*" Josie demanded, looking up in irritation once more.

Carla let loose a laugh and the full force of the hose upon Josie, all the while singing at the top of her lungs. "*A la la la la long, a la la la la long long li long long!*"

"Ah! Ma!" Josie shot up, completely soaked. "You brat! *MA!*"

Carla kept laughing as Josie ran back into the house. As the backdoor slammed shut, Carla had the sense she wasn't alone despite Josie's departure. Turning, Carla noticed a girl her age laughing right along with her just beyond the chain link fence separating their house from the one next door. The girl waved, a bright smile on her face, and Carla walked over.

"Hi! My name is Summer."

"I'm Carla. That was my sister, Josie."

"Josie's funny."

"Summer? Honey?" A deep voice came from behind Summer and Carla watched as a pair of old sneakers walked toward them. An older man crouched down into their line of vision. Small creases etched into the skin surrounding his eyes as the beginnings of middle age approached. For now, though, they still served to accentuate the happiness that spread across his face. He grinned a smile that matched Summer's, his bright white teeth standing out against tanned skin. "Well now, who is this?"

"This is Carla," said Summer.

"I just sprayed my sister with a hose," Carla informed the man proudly.

He let out a hearty chuckle. "Well Carla, it's nice to meet you."

"You too. Are you the new people?"

"Yes, we are. I met your dad just yesterday."

"Cool. Wanna come over and play? I have this hose."

"Well, I'm a little busy, but Summer and her brother can," the man said, smiling. "If it's alright with your parents, of course."

"Okay!" Carla exclaimed. She turned on her heel, splashing through her puddles and into her house to check with her parents. Josie was still angry and their mother was clearly exasperated with both of them, but Carla didn't care. She had a new friend, Summer, and together, they had the best summer.

It was in these moments, when Carla was left to her own devices, that she opened her ears and listened to the music that was playing. She could always teleport herself some other place and some other time, leaving it up to someone in her present to pull her back to reality.

Today that person was Summer, reappearing suddenly right in her face. Carla startled, the cracked green pavement and water droplets that glinted in the sunlight evaporating back into memories. "Sorry! This song always reminds me of summer as a kid."

"And, like, torturing Josie?" Summer recalled. They both snickered at the thought.

"Something like that. You wanna go?"

They exited the bookstore and Summer locked the door. She cocked her head, taking in the storefront, and sighed. "It's even dingy from the outside."

"You could paint it turquoise," Carla suggested as they set off.

"Or Fuschia. Or Liquid Gold."

"Liquid Gold? That'd definitely be a talking point."

"Naw." Summer and Carla turned the corner that would lead them to Porter Square. "It isn't even gold. It's just the name of furniture polish."

"Oh. Well, you could probably afford it then!" Carla retorted.

"Ah see? That's why I keep you around. Creative problem solving."

"I thought it was my unending sense of positivity."

"I just need to convince my mom to change some stuff. I dunno why she fights it. It'll just be me running it all eventually. If it stays open, that is. I doubt Arlo is ever gonna come back from California."

"That's gotta be nice. Right?"

"California? Yeah, if you wanna spend everything you make on rent."

"So you mean like we do here? But to live in a shitty, snowy place?"

"Touché."

"I bet you can get her to let you change it all around. You aren't even asking for much."

"You know, she doesn't like change."

"Yeah, but it's your problem to manage it, and it wasn't like it was ever your idea to open a bookstore."

"You know, you make good points…"

"Thanks."

"…when you aren't talking about yourself."

"Shut up."

The walk to Purple Salmon wasn't a long one, but the sticky June moisture had already collected in dew drops on their brows. Both women sighed in relief as they entered the air conditioned space and assumed their positions at the far end of the bar, away from the windows and hopefully away from the door, which ushered more heat and humidity in each time a new patron entered or existed.

"Hey ladies." Frankie greeted. The bartender sauntered over to them and smiled. "What can I do ya for tonight?"

"Ahem, excuse yourself?" Carla quipped at him. "That, sir, is sexual harassment."

"Ahh shoot, don't tell on me now," Frankie said, raising his hands in mock defense.

"First round's free and we'll call it even?" Carla smirked.

"I think you've failed women everywhere," Summer piped in.

"What would you like, Carla?" Frankie asked.

"Gin and tonic, please." Carla replied, though she had a feeling he already knew the answer.

"Lagunitas?"

"You got it, my friend."

A minute later, Carla and Summer were both nursing drinks. The mic up on the slightly raised stage was live and crackling as a middle-aged man took hold of it. He would be the first of the night. He strummed away at his guitar and began warbling out a halfway decent rendition of "Sister Golden Hair." After he concluded and no one else moved toward the stage, he went in for round two, warbling another tune by America. The sound was mellow and allowed Carla and Summer to continue pondering the return on investment of paint colors and mass produced pastries for the bookstore.

Several drinks and singers later, Carla pulled at her polyester pants, which had grown even more uncomfortable. She sucked down her gin and tonic through a straw. "The problem here is that the pants make me hot and this drink is very cool, but the alcohol is also very hot. I'm like a big pile of deceptive hotness."

"You sure are a big pile o' hotness."

"You get what I'm saying… The drink. It's cool, but also, it's hot."

"Better drink more of that cool drink then."

"No, no, that's not how the math problem goes. I'm hot *because* of the drink."

Summer leaned forward in silent laughter. "I'm kidding, chill out."

"No. See that's the problem. I am very, very hot right now."

"You think too much," Summer giggled uncontrollably.

The latest and greatest in guitar karaoke stepped forward. He wasn't alone though; there were other pieces who accompanied him.

"Stare much?" Summer's giggling continued.

"What? No!"

"Whatever! He's cute!"

"Yeah, you know. I guess."

"Except the suspenders. Kinda scream late

century douche."

Carla absentmindedly nodded through her haze. It was true—the performer was most likely a late century douche, but damn if he wasn't a cute one. His hair was slicked back into a topknot away from his blue eyes, which gazed out at the small crowd that had accumulated through the hours. A basic white v-neck hugged his torso and ragged grey jeans clung to his hips. A guitar was, predictably, slung across his shoulders. A repetitive drumming pattern rang through the tiny bar, followed by a bass giving off warms tones. The man stood there, not playing—not yet. Then, after a few moments more, he let a forced low husk escape his lips as he began the opening lines from The Beatles' "Come Together".

"Oh, how original," Summer snorted, taking a sip of her drink.

"But, he's *good*," Carla breathed. He kept the even pattern of the verses and gave it momentum as it rolled into the chorus and that's when he gave into his guitar, picking at it in clean lines and sweeping motions. Carla felt right on the edge as he careened over each note and word, like it would almost get away from both of them, but it never quite did. Each pick of a string landed just when it was supposed to. It was during this final riff that he looked up and across the bar, scanning the room, and found her staring. How could he not? Everyone else was fixated on whomever they came with. Carla froze, unable to look away, but eventually he did. His guitar was calling, as was the microphone.

Once the spell was broken, instinct took over. "I need to go to the bathroom."

Summer shrugged. "Okay, I got your drink."

Carla slid from her stool, surreptitiously de-clinging her pants from her butt. She was loathing them more and more by the minute. She ducked into the hallway and headed to the bathroom.

The music from the front of the house—yet

another Beatles selection—was drowned out by Michael Jackson's falsetto as he instructed everyone not to stop until they got enough.

Carla went into a stall and peeled her pants down her legs. She plunked down on the toilet with more thud than intended and rubbed her eyes. Surely they were red now—she was drowning in gin and positive it was seeping out through her pores.

The electronic beat of the eighties was getting caught in her mind, though. It called her to a time when she was in a similar state.

Her sister's wedding. It had been held a function hall roughly four miles from the house they grew up in. Josie had just married Nick Papas. They had kissed at the alter, they had smashed cake in each other's faces, they had finished walking around and thanking the two hundred and fifty family members who just *had* to be invited, and now they had collapsed in their chairs, too tired to even eat.

"Josie!" their mother shouted as she came toward them, her pink taffeta dress swishing as she moved. "You didn't even say hello to the Cassanettis!"

"Ma, I *did* say hello to them. And all your other friends," Josie assured her tiredly. Carla watched from a few tables away as Josie very deliberately and despondently spun the full champagne glass around on the table, but didn't drink from it. Carla turned to Paul, the newfound friend and only other person under fifty at their table.

"Well," Carla said, "that's why, someday, if I ever get married, I'm doing a destination wedding."

"Ha!" Paul shot her a look, blue eyes sparkling, a dimple appearing on each cheek as he smirked. "Destination wedding? Those don't exist."

"Don't exist?!"

"Well, not around here they don't. It's that," he paused, gesturing to the unhappy couple as Carla's mother dragged them across the floor to greet more people they didn't know and would never see again for the second time that night. "It's all 'the Cassanettis and the Masciarellis and the DeLucca's need to be invited! It would be a personal insult if they weren't!' And BAM! You're nailed down for a two hundred plus, three ring circus that your cousin Joey has to DJ."

"Oh, you've got it all figured out," Carla mused.

"You have no idea," Paul said. He stood, gesturing to the exit. "Wanna go for a walk?"

"Yeah. That'd be nice."

They meandered outside so that only the traces of "Build Me Up Buttercup" were sneaking their way outside. In the small, grassed area masquerading as a courtyard, they sat on a bench, and Carla, unsure what to do next, looked up at the white lights hanging from the terrace. She could feel Paul's eyes on her.

"Cigar?" he offered. Carla glanced at him, unsure, and he smiled again. "Ever smoked one?"

"No."

"Do you wanna?"

"I don't see any. Euphemism?"

"No!" Paul laughed, extracting one out from a small box by his side. "Get your mind out of the gutter."

"Sorry," Carla said, feeling her cheeks color. "You know what Freud said…"

"I know what he said about everything else," Paul said as he lit the cigar and inhaled slightly, letting the smoke escape from his mouth almost immediately.

Well, this time he said, 'sometimes a cigar is just a cigar'."

Carla took the cigar from Paul, but inhaled too deeply, choking a bit. She passed it back to him, smacking the taste from her lips. "Ugh! God, that's terrible."

Paul snuffed the cigar out and rested it on the

edge of the bench, returning his focus to Carla. "In that case, this time Freud was wrong."

He pulled her close, pressing their mouths together in a deep kiss.

As Carla was currently not sitting on a bench in a faux courtyard, but in a bathroom with a questionable level of cleanliness, the spell cast by the music was easily broken as the toilet auto-flushed before she had even stood up. She snapped to in a lame attempt to avoid splash back. As if getting her sweaty work pants back on wasn't already enough of a chore. She banged around in the stall, trying to unlatch it, and eventually gave up. Throwing all her weight against the door while jamming her hand against the slider, she fell out of it and practically collided with Summer.

"Woah there, you okay?"

"Yeah, I just got a little stuck."

"Right."

"Did you need the stall?"

"No, I just came to check on you. That singer guy is done; he's a couple seats down the bar from us."

"Okay."

Summer rolled her eyes at Carla, "Just come on."

Carla followed Summer back out to reclaim their spots. Just as she'd said, the singer was just two seats away.

"Frankie, can I get another?" Carla asked.

"Sure can." Frankie took stock of her empty glass, then looked in the mystery singer guy's direction. "And what can I get you, boss?"

The singer was lounging back in his chair, looking through his phone, and Frankie's voice caught him off guard. He looked up quickly and, pointing to Carla's glass, asked, "Um, what going in there?"

"Gin and Tonics," she replied.

This got a smile out of him, "Tonics? Huh, I'm gonna go with Jameson on the rocks."

"You got it." Frankie went to work, leaving Carla and Jameson on the Rocks with open air between them.

"I usually only drink whiskey."

Carla rarely knew what the right thing to say in any situation was. On this occasion, she went with, "I usually only drink clear alcohols."

"Oh, okay," he said with a shrug. He held out his hand. "Nico."

"Carla," she said, taking it. "Have you been here before?"

"Only a couple times. I just moved out of Allston to this part of town."

"Gotcha. You work around here?"

"Actually, Berklee, for grad school."

"Oh," Carla pushed the words from her body, "nice."

Summer, as if on cue, spurted out, "Carla used to go there!"

"Oh, you did!"

Here we go, thought Carla, and said, "Yeah, I studied music."

"Oh really? Sick, what do you do now?"

Carla had to once again take stock of herself. "I work Downtown."

"Cool. Cool."

"So bongos?"

He smiled sheepishly. "Yeah, well, are you gonna lug a drum kit to an open mic night?"

"As it happens, I've always felt that Cuban hand drums were the one element The Beatles were missing."

"Really?"

"Naw, but I'm four gin and tonics in and I'm doing my best."

Nico let a small laugh escape through his smile and he stood up. "I should get back to my friends, but it was nice meeting you, Carla." With that, he disappeared into a small crowd of people that had been slowly building.

"'It was nice to meet you'," quoted Summer. "How about that?"

"How about what?" Carla said, wide-eyed despite knowing exactly what her friend was getting at.

"You know," Summer teased. Her eyes were fully bloodshot and she rocked back, erupting in gales of laughter.

"Stop. Just don't, he probably meets, like, a hundred people a night."

"I saw you looking at him while he played, you creep."

"I'm not a creep, you're a creep." Cara guffawed back. "I think maybe we need to make these drinks our last?"

"You don't sound committed."

"I'm a very committed person. I'm committed to not wearing these crappy pants."

"Huh."

"I want to take off my pants!" Carla declared and, with that, realized just how loud she was speaking; some people were even staring. "Hey, Summer?"

"Yeah?"

"What do you think the over-under is that Nico just heard me?"

"Probably pretty good, he's walking over now."

"Damn it."

"Lighten up, nerd."

"Hey," Nico said to the back of Carla's head. She continued to look straight forward.

"Yeah?" She said still looking at Summer.

"We're all taking off, but I was hoping to get your number first."

Carla spun around, aghast anyone would've asked such a question. Such a pedestrian request and there it sat before her. She had met a human man in a bar and he wanted her number. How old fashioned. "Yeah. Here, call yourself." She handed her phone over to him and watched with great interest as she internalized the fact she had met a man outside of the world of Tinder.

"Cool." He handed her phone back over to her. "I'll see you around." Nico walked off.

"Yeah, see you." She looked at Summer. "Did you see that?"

"Nico getting your number?"

"Yeah, I think I might be having an out-of-body experience. It's like the olden days."

"Like how our parents met?"

"Yeah." Carla finished the rest of her drink in one gulp. "I think I'm officially cooked."

"I think you're officially cooked too."

And with that, they duo dumped some cash on the bar and slid from their stools. The air outside now was far cooler than before, despite the atmosphere still retaining a good deal of clamminess still clinging to the air. Carla's face, however, was screaming with heat. It could've been the alcohol. It could've been the Nico.

ON YOUR FEET

Carla thumped her foot into Summer and Jas' solid wooden door, making a repetitive *thwak* sound. It creaked open and a sleepy Summer peered out at her.

"Hemmfy ldaadddfyy"

"Good morning, Carla?" She held out a hand and Carla opened her mouth, releasing the brown paper bag.

"You said ten!"

"Is it ten?"

"There're bagels in there."

Summer considered this. "In that case, come in, come in."

"What'd you do last night?"

"I'm honestly just still really tired from Friday."

"That was the day before yesterday!"

"We can't all be blessed with hollow legs like you."

"Twenty-five isn't looking so good on you these days." Carla passed through the threshold.

"Not right now anyway." Summer shut the door behind her. "After you went home, Jas had some friends over, we wound up just staying up all night and the rest is history."

"Well, you're holding the bagels," she set the hot cups in her hand down on the table, "and here are the coffees. My work here is done." She collapsed on the couch.

Summer released the bag from her hand, letting it land next to the coffees and flopped onto the couch beside Carla, who wound up with Summer's feet on her lap. "Why is this happening to me?"

"I think you already answered that one, grandma."

"Shut up." Summer rolled onto her back and propped her head up on a pillow so that her eyes were pointing at Carla. "What'd you do with your Saturday? I spent mine trying and failing to eat Chinese food."

"Mostly goofing off, a little writing."

"You wrote? Music or lyrics?"

"Music."

"Look at you. You haven't said that in a while."

"I mean it isn't anything special, I was just plucking away at some strings."

"You should share it with Jas, he always wants someone to do music stuff with. Like, besides his bandmates."

"Yeah, maybe."

Summer rolled her eyes and then immediately winced in pain at the action, "So that's a hard *no* then."

"Oh, don't be like that! Where's Jas anyway?"

"Sleeping, lucky shit."

"Want me to fix that?"

"Not unless you want to die at the tender age of twenty-five."

"It's getting less tender by the day."

"I dunno about that, I'm feeling pretty tender right now."

"You're feeling pretty hung over right now."

"Eh, whatever. New topic. Did you get a call from

anyone in particular?" Summer asked, waggling her brows.

"Don't be creepy."

Summer jabbed her foot into the side of Carla's leg. "I'm not creepy. Everyone makes suggestive eyebrows when asking about potential—"

"Potential *nothings*." Carla cut in. She grabbed Summer's foot and started tickling it. "Two can play at that game, my friend. I have serious allergies and I can't smell your stinky feet, so joke's on you."

"Ah! Stop!" Summer started laughing uncontrollably and wiggling around. In an attempt to make the tickling end, Summer sat up out of reflex and swung an arm wildly at the back of Carla's neck, trying to get her in a headlock. Due to lack of flexibility, it was a failed attempt and she wound up smacking Carla on the back

"Who do you think you are? Hulk Hogan?"

Summer tried again, this time grabbing at Carla's hand and wrenching it back, causing them both to bend into awkward angles. "He was a criminally underrated wrestler whose talent in the ring was overshadowed by an aptly cultivated Hollywood persona!" Summer choked out.

"Oh my God," Carla struggled and writhed further, "for the last time," they both rolled off the couch with a plunk onto the floor, "I don't watch the WWE and I don't know what that means."

"Ouch!" Summer released Carla and exhaled, laughing, "Truce! Truce!"

Carla mirrored the release and laughed, "Truce!" She held her hands up.

"Okay." A deep rumble reverberated through the room, "you win, I'm awake."

"Oops."

Jas, Summer's husband, came ambling out of their room, sleepy and disgruntled. He dragged his feet across the floor. Each step vibrated through the planks of wood, announcing his approach. He plopped onto the armrest of the couch and allowed his upper body to fall back. He wiggled a bit until he could get comfortable.

"Well," Jas said after a minute of silence, "you might as well talk now, I'm up."

"Carla gave her number to a boy."

"What Summer means is that there's coffee and food on the table for you if you want," Carla said. She slid out from between the couch and coffee table, repositioning herself on the floor with her legs propped up against a chair that sat to the side on a Dutch angle.

"That's my coffee!" Summer shouted, her head popping up.

"Not any more, traitor."

Jas tipped himself onto one side and reached a lanky, long arm over to a coffee. "Mine now," he shoved a pillow under his head to keep it propped up and attempted a sip. "So Carla."

"So Jas."

"Tell me about your new man."

"I see why you two are married."

Summer peered over, "It's a harmless question."

"Yeah Carla, it's a harmless question," Jas retorted.

"I've heard nothing from him."

"Classic early-century-douche move."

"His name is Nico."

"Nico?" Jas asked, his face contorting in distaste, "Gross."

"Stop now."

Summer laughed, "You like him."

"I don't care."

"If you didn't, you wouldn't be saying so. You'd just not care."

"No."

"When'd you meet *Nico?*" Jas asked, slurping his coffee.

"Oh, you mean the guy I'm not talking to?"

"She met him Friday night."

"Friday?"

"Yeah, but I don't know why we're talking about this. He's just a guy in a bar."

"Chill out. It's only been two days."

Carla pulled her feet back off the couch and sat up, grabbing at the bag, "I'm not wound up. There's no chilling necessary." She pulled a bagel out of the bag. "And how would you even know? You two met when you were, like, twenty and moved in with each other four months later."

"Well, we aren't that much out of the game," Summer crawled on all fours toward the bagel. "And you can't eat that." She swiped it from Carla's hand.

"And why not?"

"It's Sunday. Sunday means it's your family dinner-lunch thing."

"Maybe I'll eat two dinners?"

"You won't," Summer said. She took a bite and continued through a mouthful of bagel, "You know if you don't eat enough, your mom will start interrogating you."

"Fine, you're probably right." Carla looked despondently at the fallen sesame seed soldier. "Wanna just watch TV?"

"What'd'ya wanna watch?" Jas asked as he dug around the couch. Eventually, he produced a remote and hit the power button. The television whined and buzzed for a minute before producing an image. A man with a strong jawline sat behind a table and projected multisyllabic words at them with a smooth, deep voice.

"Not news."

Jas plopped the remote onto Summer's lap and gulped some more coffee. "Your problem now."

Hey Carla, what'd'ya wanna watch?"

"I don't care. Anything about something far away from here."

Summer busied herself by clicking through channels while Carla squiggled her body around into a comfortable position. She boosted her head up from a pillow she snagged from a disgruntled Jas and pointed her eyes in the direction of the television.

Hours flew by as they rearranged themselves into more comfortable positions, got up to grab more snacks or took a bathroom break. Jas mentioned a song contest he wanted to enter, while Summer pondered how she would ever convince her parents to make her espresso-infused changes to the bookstore. Carla nodded, and gave vocal recognition to their thoughts throughout, but when conversation stalled and all that filled the void were the sounds from the whining television, Carla couldn't help thinking about her unfilled quotas at work, her unfilled notebook at home, and the guy she had met Friday who hadn't yet called her.

The door swung open and Carla stepped inside. Creaky floor boards were always what greeted her first. *Thump, thump, thump*. Her dad was digging his heels into the floor with each step one floor above. The muffled wail of Celine Dion filled in the spaces left open from clanging pots in the kitchen. Straight down the hallway and beyond the kitchen she could see out to the backyard. Her sister's children ran in circles, yelping. Carla slowly stepped down the hall listening to the percussion of footsteps and pots mixing with the melody of screaming children and a pining Celine. The soundtrack of her home.

"Ma?" she called as she arrived in the kitchen. "Do you need help?"

The only thing remotely linking Carla to her mother via appearance was the plume of unruly curls that sprouted from her mother's head. Carla had discovered the power of smoothing oils, but her mother had not. As the fifty-five-year-old woman straightened up, removing her head from the oven, the humidity and heat had zeroed in on her twisted strands, making them explode in a messy halo.

"Well, not now. You're about twenty minutes too late. I could've used you on the gravy," her mother said, placing the baked ziti on the stovetop. "You must be related to your father." She opened her arms, into which Carla slumped lazily.

"Good, it's about a thousand degrees in here anyway." Her mother's grip on her was tight, and while some may have found the hug aggressive, Carla always found it comforting. Eventually her mom released her.

"You can always go outside with the kids," she said, motioning to the little boy and girl belonging to Carla's sister.

"Well, Josie never wanted to play with the hose with me, but maybe they will."

"Oh, don't remind me," her mother groaned, raking her hand through her hair in an attempt to manage the mess. "Every summer she'd be tanning and you'd be squirting her with that hose."

"She here now?"

"No, she dropped the kids off this morning before her shift. She should be here soon though."

Carla continued, "How's Dad?"

"Good. He's in a good mood today."

"Good, good." Carla looked to the bare table. "Here." She walked to a cabinet and extracted some plates. "Nick coming tonight?"

"No, no Nick today."

"Josie isn't gonna like that," Carla muttered as she put one plate back in the cabinet.

"So, Miss Carla," her mother finally sat on a kitchen chair, giving her feet a break. "What is going on in your world?"

"Um…" As Carla set each plate down, the clomp of solid wood confirmed their position. "You know, just same old, same old. I visited Summer at the bookstore the other day."

"Oh, really?" Her mother's attention was caught. The woman basically lived off of meatballs and idle gossip. "You know, I saw her mother next door the other day. She said they're thinking of selling."

Carla thought back to her visit. "It was kinda slow when I was in there. Summer's thinking they should—"

"—open a coffee shop? Her mother mentioned that too."

"Well, no. Not open a coffee shop, just add one."

"Ha. Gonna take more than coffee to save that place."

"People like that stuff." Carla opened a drawer and took out silverware.

"Who would wanna go to an old bookstore in the back alleys of Cambridge and drink a crappy cup of coffee. I mean, Summer—bless her soul—can't cook. You two used to always make a mess in here." She smiled at the memory.

"A. You'd be surprised. People love back alley shit—"

"Watch that mouth, Carla."

"—and B. We were like, eleven. I'm sure she can brew a cup of coffee now."

"When was the last time you had coffee with her?"

"This morning, in fact."

"Okay, and who made it?"

"Dunkin' Donuts, but that's not the point."

"Well, I guess we can say you're a good friend."

"It's a good idea. Hipsters love going to rundown places and paying too much to exist there. It's a thing, I swear."

"What's a hip-ster?" her mother began to ask, but was thankfully interrupted by the bellowing voice of father.

"Ana!" Joe was calling from upstairs. "Ana?"

"WHAT?" her mother hollered back at him.

"ANA!" he called again, louder this time. A career spent in construction had left the sixty-two-year-old slightly hearing impaired, to say the least.

"Jesus, Mary, and Joseph… I swear," Ana sighed. She leaned on her knees, depending on inertia to help her up. She roamed out of the kitchen and down the hallway to the stairs. "WHAT?"

"Have you seen the shirt?"

"What shirt?"

"The shirt! You know!"

"The green button down?"

"Yeah! The one I wear every Sunday! Hello, duh?"

"It's hanging in your closet. Right where it always is."

Carla could hear him stomping back into their bedroom right as the squeak of a front door opening joined the procession of shouting voices.

"Ma?"

"You moved it!"

"Hi, Josie, sweetie," their mother greeted before turning back to the stairs, "And no I didn't, it's right where it always is!"

"What's he looking for?" Josie asked.

"My green shirt! Your mother's always hiding things from me!"

"No, I'm not!"

"Why does he always wear that shirt?" Josie asked in a whisper.

"You got me," her mother whisper-mumbled.

"It's a good shirt!"

"It's a wonderful shirt, honey," Ana shouted back up at him. "It's an okay shirt," she mumbled back at Josie.

"It's Sunday, I like to wear a collar."

The two women were already walking back into the kitchen. "But it's—"

"Just let him have his thing."

"But it's an old, worn-out shirt—"

"It's a thing, just let him have the thing," Ana repeated, clearly done with the conversation. Josie stopped short at the sight of Carla setting the table.

"Oh," Josie said, "you're here already."

"That okay?"

"Yeah, of course. I'm just surprised is all," Josie said. She peaked into the side room. "Where are Joey and Antonietta?"

"Outside," Carla said, pointing to the yard.

"Oh," Josie murmured. Her eyes refocused. "Well then, why don't I see them?"

"Huh?"

"Carla, where are they?"

"I don't know. They're in the yard playing. They probably ran around the house or something."

"*Jesus*," Josie hissed, tromping outside. "Joey!"

"Ma!" a little voice hollered out.

"Get in here."

"She's chasing me, Ma!" the voice returned. The children's giggles got louder.

"See? They're on the side of the house. It's fine."

"No, it's not fine. You won't get it until you have kids."

"I get it *fine*," Carla mocked. "You had kids and then forgot everything we used to do and how we'd be fine every time anyway."

"I don't know *what* you're talking about," Josie said, raising her eyebrows, indicating to their mother, who was standing just a few feet away.

Carla grinned and raised her eyebrows as well. "Really, you don't?" She grabbed a piece of bread out of a bowl her mother was placing on the table.

"What? Remember what?" their mother piped in. She was an auditory bloodhound.

"Ma! Antonietta got me!" Joey called, providing a reprieve from a now overly interested Ana. Joey entered the house through the sliding back door, drenched.

Josie's mouth fell open while Carla's widened into a smile.

"Look at you little man, you're soaked!" Carla said. Joey giggled in reply.

"Antonietta! Look at what you did to your brother!" Josie cried.

The seven-year-old stepped forward with a smirk on her lips, just as wet. "Sorry, Ma."

"I guess we know who you take after."

"The better sister?" Carla suggested, chomping down on the bread.

"Here's hoping she gets it together sooner than you do," Josie muttered as she grabbed Joey's hand.

"Hey!" Carla pinched her big sister. It was still easy to get under her skin.

"Ouch!" Josie pinched Carla back.

"Ha! Ouch," Carla laughed. "I still got it."

"What's all this fuss about?" asked her father, who had finally managed to join them downstairs. He was outfitted in his finest green button down. Carla knew the bottom was fraying as he had had it for so many years, but so long as the fray was tucked into his pants, it may as well have been a brand-new shirt.

"She got me all wet!" Joey proudly announced as Josie dragged him back towards the front of the house.

"All wet?"

"Yeah, I got him!" Antonietta confirmed proudly as she followed after her brother and mother.

"No, no. You stay down here young lady. Go play with your auntie. I'm raising the second coming of her, apparently," Josie tossed over her shoulder. "Dad, I'm gonna have to steal one of your t-shirts for Joey while his clothes dry off!"

Antonietta shrugged and galloped back into the kitchen and sat next to Carla, looking up at her with big brown eyes.

"That's fine," their dad yelled up through the

ceiling. He hobbled to the radio and twisted the old nobs, pulling the sound away from the CD setting and onto the radio. Celine's tale of driving all night was cut short in lieu of the oldies found on WZLX.

Carla could still hear the mother-son exchange as they walked upstairs.

"Honestly, look at you."

"I know! Look at me."

"You always let her do this."

"I should probably get her back."

Josie let out a sigh, "Yeah… Wait, what? I mean, no!"

"Whatcha doing?" Antonietta's voice broke into Carla's eavesdropping. She looked down at her niece's dimpled and mischievous face.

"I s'pose I should be folding napkins while Nona puts the food on the table, shouldn't I?"

Antonietta nodded very knowingly.

"Great! Glad you agree. You are the lucky winner who gets to help me!"

"Aw man!"

"That's aw *woman* to you."

Antonietta let out a big sigh. "Fine."

"Yeah, I know." Carla placed a stack of paper napkins in front of them and grabbed one. "Fold and repeat, my friend."

Eventually Josie and Joey reappeared downstairs with Josie looking ever the more tired at each passing minute and Joey looking ever the more pleased that he got to wear one of Nonno's white undershirts. Everyone's butt found a seat, the perfunctory thank yous were sent to the big guy upstairs, and Carla could finally dig into her meal in peace.

"So, how's work going?" A very brief moment of peace.

"Fine, Ma."

"Uh huh, that's good. And have you been seeing

anyone lately?"

Carla smiled at her mother. "Well, I just told you how I saw Summer today."

"That's not what I meant."

"Oh, sorry, Jas was there too."

"Ma, give it up," Josie piped in with an eyeroll.

"Josephine, don't *Ma* me."

"I've been really busy."

"What about that guy?"

Carla sat on alert and asked, "What guy?" She could swear her mother could smell it on her when she was ever thinking about anyone.

"You were seeing him a while ago."

"Who've you ever brought around other than Pau—" Josie cut in, but Carla kicked her under the table.

"I haven't been seeing anyone and thanks a lot," Carla assured the table. Her father was tuned out, busy shoveling meatballs into his mouth. Carla wished everyone else would follow suit.

"Hey!" Josie kicked her back.

"Can't you see us right now?" Joey piped up.

"Ouch! Yeah, buddy, I can see you guys right now," Carla mumbled, focused on spearing a ziti.

"Paul!" her mother shouted victoriously.

"I never brought Paul around. He just existed near you all."

Her mother was abuzz. "What does that mean? Josie, what is your sister talking about?"

Josie rolled her eyes. "He was at our wedding, remember? He was Nick's friend from, like, high school."

"There you go, that's why you think I brought him around. I didn't though, he was just around for other reasons."

"But you carried on with him."

"Yeah, Ma," Carla said around a mouthful of ziti, praying the interrogation would end.

"Well, why couldn't you make it work? He has a

good job."

"I think there needs to be more there than that. I mean, I have a good job."

"A debt collector?"

"It pays the bills." Carla tried not to think about Guccibear and how if she didn't reel him in, she'd be waiting tables soon.

"But Carla," her mother lowered her voice, preparing everyone for the negative statement that was to follow, "people don't like debt collectors."

"Really? I thought debt collections was ranked right under Mother Theresa in terms of popular opinion."

"Don't be smart with me."

"Can we just eat?"

Her mother dipped a chunk of bread into gravy and threw it in her mouth, an air of frustration about her. Calypso influenced beats from "Brown-Eyed Girl" bounded towards her as the noise emanating from the radio was all that remained. This house, her parents and sister, they were all sitting around in their time capsule eating dinners from yesteryear. Van Morrison was screaming his la-la-las out to the heavens.

She was propped up in the passenger seat of her dad's Chevy Nova. Her dad never used the air conditioning—too much gas—opting to roll the windows down instead. This was always better in Carla's opinion since they could sing as loud as they wanted and neither could hear the other one. If there was one thing Carla had learned by the age of nine, it was that she loved singing at the top of her lungs.

"Sha la la la!" they both yelled in unison.

Her dad had continued down Route One and they both looked at each other before opening their mouths to below out some more *la las*. After their rousing chorus finished, Carla rested her head on the back of the seat and concentrated as the Golden Banana passed them by.

"You love your singing, don't you, kiddo?" her dad chuckled.

"Um, I dunno." She was always a little bashful. "I guess so."

"You guess so? I think you like it. You're always belting it out whenever you can."

Carla kicked one sneaker into the other; they lit up for a minute before going dark.

"Well, you should sing more then," her dad continued.

"I should?"

"Yeah, if you like doing it."

"I just like the sound of music."

"You like it when Uncle Jimmy plays the guitar?"

"Yes!" Carla exclaimed, suddenly perking up. "I love the sound it makes."

"Well, maybe he can teach you to play a little."

"You really think so?"

"Yeah, I'll just ask him to bring it when he comes around for Sunday dinner."

"Hm. Okay."

"No. Not, 'Hm okay.' Definitely okay. Just make sure you learn at least one thing."

"At least one thing?"

"Yeah, every time you wanna learn anything, you don't have to be perfect at first. Just walk away and try and remember one new thing."

"Yessir."

"Good. That's what I like to hear."

Her dad ran his right palm over the rubber steering wheel and tapped his thumb against it, now thinking deeply. "Did you know Uncle Jimmy used to be in a band?"

"Nope!"

"Yeah, he could play the hell outta that guitar."

"Where'd the band go?"

"Well, you know, he got… just… caught up."

"What was he caught in?"

"Just life. He needed money. When you're older, you need that. So, I got him a job in construction with me."

"So, does Uncle Jimmy not like his life all that much?"

"What? God no, He has his own family now. He's happy. But Carla, I'm just saying, if you have a dream, don't let that go, okay?"

"His band was his dream?"

"Yeah, and he gave it all up. Just for some money. Just to bust his ass a little and make someone else a lot."

"Couldn't he just go back?"

"The older you get, the harder that is."

"So does Uncle Jimmy not like his life all that much?"

"What? God no, He has his own family now. He's happy. But Carla, I'm just saying, if you have a dream you don't let that go, okay?"

"Okay."

"Once it goes, it ain't coming back."

"Okay, I promise."

The two fell into silence.

Her father was the first to break it, fearful they had taken a turn too serious. "So, Carla?"

"Yeah, Dad?"

"You know we have to be back for dinner," he said, glancing over at her.

"Yeah," she conceded. Her little shoulders slumped. They had made a quick escape to Winthrop where they'd stolen a few moments watching the airplanes land. The airplanes came in quick and close over their heads. Another perfect place to sing so no one could hear you.

"Well, what if," he whispered, a secretive smile on

his lips, "we got some ice cream first?"

Carla's eyes brightened. "Yes, yes, yes!"

"Okay, okay!" he laughed. "But you know the deal."

"Don't tell Mom!"

"And?"

"And I gotta stuff all the food at dinner into my belly."

"Right. Cause otherwise she'll know. Then she'll get mad at me for giving you dessert before dinner and your sister'll get jealous you got ice cream."

"I promise."

Awhile after pulling off Route One, they were eating their soft serve ice cream. The twist flavor—it always had to be the twist because why would you just have chocolate or vanilla when you could have both? Carla destroyed her cone, smearing most of it on her face in the process. Her dad laughed as he cleaned her up, running through their cover up plan once more with Carla as he did so.

Later that night, her mother sat and watched Carla with suspicion as she painstakingly swallowed bite after bite of chicken. Carla was committed to the plan and her father snuck her winking encouragements whenever his wife wasn't looking. Josie rolled her eyes, but kept her mouth shut, as she too had once upon a time gone to watch the planes with Dad and eaten ice cream too close to dinner before returning home.

At this moment, Carla would've loved to be able to shrink back into the little girl who ate ice cream before dinner and regretted it. If life was a meal, she skipped the school, too impatient, and dove into working, into making money. She had face-planted into dessert. At least when she was small, she had a temporary bellyache and that was the end of that. She pulled an Uncle Jimmy and cut her losses. As an adult…

But here she sat now, with a disgruntled mother, nervous for her aging daughter's security and a failed brief from her father. As the years wore away at him, the smiles and winks he once gave carved rivulets into his face. Her once jovial, dreamy, mischievous father had morphed into a paranoid, concerned, and overly cautious parent.

"What's the dream boat thinking of?" her dad asked with smirk. He still made an effort to soften his newfound edges from time to time.

"Work. See there was this guy with a—"

"Are you still thinking of staying with that job?" her mother interjected.

"Um, yep. That was the plan," Carla said. She knew the trajectory her mother would've preferred her young daughter take.

"What kind of job is that, though?" her mother prodded, expressing her disapproval for the second time that night.

"The kind that pays my bills."

"And makes you a pariah to the general public?"

"Josephine, don't call your sister a pariah," Ana interjected.

"Pariah, isn't that a fish!" Antonietta piped up.

"No, sweetie," Josie cooed, "that's a piranha."

"It's fine, Ma, I know I'm a pariah. If you know you're a pariah, then you've really outsmarted the people calling you a pariah."

"What's a piranha look like?" Antonietta asked, ignoring her aunt and grandmother.

"Don't call yourself something like that, Carla!"

"Josie called me that first…" Carla responded.

Joe leaned back in his chair and rubbed his eyes. This wasn't the conversation he'd intended to start.

"Uhm," Josie reached around behind her, searching for her phone.

"Couldn't you be a teacher or something?" Ana suggested. "People love teachers."

"…I just happened to add to her argument," Carla continued.

"God, where did my phone go?" Josie looked around distracted.

"People love teachers." Her mother sliced her utensils through her food.

"People also like to be able to make rent every month."

"Ha! Got it." Josie brought the phone around.

"I know what a piranha is!" Joey burst out with. "Tommy Ciotinelli said he saw one once!"

This brought the conversation to a halt.

"Really?" Josie asked, raising a skeptical eyebrow. "And where did Tommy Ciotinelli see this piranha?"

"He was on a boat and then his uncle threw a huge fish in the water," Joey recalled. "All of a sudden a piranha came out of nowhere and…" Joey wiggled and writhed around as if he was being eaten by a piranha.

Josie let out an exasperated sigh and mumbled, "I suppose he was boating down the Charles, too."

"It did happen!"

Antonietta cackled in her chair. "Tommy's a liar!"

"No," Joey's face became red as he grew more defensive. "No, it happened!"

Ana's momentary lapse in attention returned. "You could go back to school, Carla."

"Ana," Joe warned.

"Ma, if I go back to school, I'd finish studying music."

"You want to be a music teacher? Well, they don't make anything."

To Carla's left, the sibling rivalry raged on with Joey and Antonietta engaging in a tennis match of *yeah-hahs* and *nuh-uhs*.

"But she could have a nice steady paycheck and

her summers off, and, you know…" Ana looked dreamily at her two grandchildren in the midst of an important battle over whether or not Tommy Ciotinelli had, in fact, watched a piranha eat a fish before his eyes. Joey had begun a rousing reenactment in which he was the piranha, and his sister, was the fish.

"Oh… Oh ho. No, I don't think so," Carla assured her. She could barely watch Joey and Antoinetta for an afternoon, let alone a full classroom of children like them.

"What?" Her mother feigned bewilderment.

"Do you want to be a teacher?" Joe asked.

"No." Easy question. Easy answer.

"You wanna be a debt collector?"

"Oh, don't say it like that, Joe" her mother sighed, scrunching up her nose at the sound of the words. "*Debt collector*. Ugh."

"Well, what do I really want?"

She avoided thinking about the question even to herself. It was painful to admit an answer that in her gut was a faint dream she knew would never come true.

"She obviously wants to be a song–"

"Debt collection makes me money," Carla said, cutting off Josie. "I know it depends on how much debt I collect, but I collect it."

"Sure, Carla, reach for the stars."

"Carla's smart," Joe said. "She's got a good job, she knows her business, and it isn't like it's ever gonna leave her broke or injured." He looked to his right leg, which was stuck out from under the table a bit straighter than the left.

"Yeah, it's fine for her to pay her bills, but it isn't what she actually wants to do every day," Josie continued. "She started school at Be—"

"Carla," Joe cut in, looking right at her, "don't be stupid. You've got a good job, right? You can't put a price on security."

"No, I guess I can't, can I?" Carla looked at her food, thinking back to her sunny day in the car with her dad years ago.

"But teachers get *pensions*," her mother added helpfully.

"Ma, I *don't* want to be a teacher," Carla said. She speared absentmindedly waved a forkful of ziti forcefully, ending the conversation.

"It just seems like a shame."

"It's a shame, alright," said Josie.

Carla plopped one foot in front of the other as she walked home. The pavement was cracked and lumpy, and she didn't move across it so much as it flowed beneath her. Walking the same streets for so many years made them pass by like nothing. Eventually, she turned the corner at a chain-linked fence that had shrubs exploding out of it, arriving on her street. She inhabited the middle unit of a triple-decker that had been sliced into a million pieces. More apartments meant more money, so while a two-bedroom had largely swallowed up her floor, she had managed to claim a bizarrely-shaped studio. As she walked up the wooden steps, she was careful to place her feet on the left side where they creaked less and to skip the middle step. A chunk of the wood had broken through several months ago and Norm, her landlord, couldn't be bothered to fix it. To be fair, the tenants could've cared less to make him; unrepaired stairs kept rent low.

She unlocked the door and entered her abode, though calling it humble would've been generous. Fewer things had brought horror to her parent's faces than when Carla announced she would be paying someone money each month to live in two hundred and fifty square feet a mile away from her childhood home. It was unfathomable to them that she wouldn't rather continue living with them as she had through her first and only year of college.

The floors were smooth hardwood, she had a bed pushed up against the window at the front, and the mini-fridge and microwave that masqueraded as a kitchen flowed through to the back of her unit, which featured a windowless bathroom. Artwork was thrown hastily on her walls. It wasn't a palace, but it hit her price range and all she needed to live at the end of the day was a place to sleep, play her guitar, and a freezer full of ice cream sandwiches. She threw the leftovers her mother had insisted she take home into the fridge and roamed over to her bed, collapsing into the sheets.

The day hadn't been a total bust. Sure, she got the typical career slam-down, but in the end, who had Uncle Sam chasing them down and who was doing the chasing? Of course, the fact that her mother would always be enamored with her sister's ability to pump out two kids was another persistent jab. Still, she had well over a decade of solid procreation potential left, so how bad off could she be? Her morning had still been mellow and she had managed to walk out the door with enough food for at least two dinners.

She sat up and grabbed her guitar from the bed where she had lazily dropped it before going out that morning and lamely plucked at some strings. She strummed a G chord and sent some warm, cozy sounds throughout her room. Too warm though. C was lower and grumpier; it flew out more naturally from her fingers and, for that matter, her heart.

The guitar couldn't hold her attention though, and she set it back in its home on its stand. Walking to her fridge, she opened it and stared at the leftovers on the bottom and the ice cream up top. That was of no interest to her either. She was full. Too full for ice cream sandwiches, even on a soupy day such as this one. She stared at the TV, but didn't even bother. It was no use. She didn't want to admit it; she hated to be this person. But her phone hadn't gone off and it had piled onto a dip in an otherwise mellow mood.

Sinking back into her bed once more, she reached a hand into her bag and removed a phone from it. Summer, always the patient one, was always quite willing to listen to her every whim, but she didn't even know exactly what to whine about. Her fingers hovered above the screen poised to type… something.

I

Okay, good start. Now, for the rest of what was presumably going to come out as an infantile complaint. But *what* infantile complaint?

I'm over this; Nico should've called me by now.

But that didn't even make sense. If she was over it, why would she be texting about it?

I can't believe he didn't text me.

Also a lie, no one met in bars in real life, swapped numbers, and actually dated. Or hooked up. Or anything. Not anymore.

Her phone lit up before she could type something new. Aghast, she sat up and clicked into the message. She needn't text Summer, because Summer was texting her.

Yo you wanna come back over? Dinner must be over with by now. I swear I'm functional.

Fair enough—Carla just assumed complain in person. She clicked into the text box, vaguely aware of the screen flashing with a new text, and absentmindedly thumbed *sure* in response. After hitting send, Carla noticed the new text hadn't been another from Summer, but from Nico.

Hey, if you wanna hang out, I'm around now, I'm about to make dinner.

And that *sure* she had already sent had gone into their new chat conversation rather than to Summer. Aghast, Carla tossed her phone away into the sheets in surprise, instant regret pooling in the pit of her stomach. Her respond would come off as too quick, totally overeager. Not only that, but their first time hanging out beyond the bar would be at Nico's apartment—alone.

On the other hand, Carla didn't like to play games, so what was wrong with such a quick response? Then again, always cutting to the chase could have been what led to her constant state of singledom and train wreck relationship endings…

Cool, Carla thought. She sighed, trying to bring herself back from her internal spiral. Then, another ping from her phone. She retrieved it gingerly, glancing at the screen. Nico, providing his address. Not so slow to respond himself. Maybe this was the beginning to something that would be remotely adult-like.

Everyone in the western world might frown at a first-time apartment visit, but Carla was armed with some ill-acquired pepper spray and Nico didn't look too formidable, so she figured too much couldn't go wrong. She launched herself from the bed and ripped off the clothes she'd worn around her parent's house, choosing instead to don her emergency underwear, a string top, and a skirt. She'd been in a dry spell and that needed to be amended.

Even if she was just walking into a booty call, that would be absolutely fine. Carla's love life had, for quite a while, largely consisted of a drawn out expanse of Paul punctuated by other men and stints of alone time. She left that behind shortly after imploding, and she'd vowed that the next morning to never have repeat performance.

It was a short walk to the T and an even shorter ride to Davis Square. As she walked down the bike path and looked at some people walking their dogs and other people walking their children, she came to a large and colorfully painted structure. She took an abrupt left. It was an odd location for Nico. This was a pricey zip code and he'd said he was a student. She turned right down a different street and walked past triple-deckers. They had clearly been fixed up recently, possibly by the same owner. The houses were old, but all gleamed with uniform updates. Carla counted house numbers and vaguely wondered if he had roommates. There was no way one student could afford a place on his own. Definitely not one this nice. The number counting brought her just past the triple-deckers though and right to a brick building, an even newer-looking apartment complex. She looked down at her phone and back at the number on the building. She'd arrived.

Carla punched her finger against Nico's buzzer, which pierced annoying pinholes into her eardrums. She received a second buzz in response and heard the lock click. She wrenched the front door open and took her time walking up the stairs. His door was in a corner and, as Carla went to knock, it swung open before she could even have the chance.

Nico stood in front of her in a wife beater and lived-in khaki shorts. He held out an arm to usher her inside and removed a fedora from his head. It struck Carla as odd that someone would wear a hat indoors while by himself, but gave it a pass regardless and took his arm.

"Glad you made it," Nico said with a smile.

"Yeah, thanks for shooting me a text."

Carla stepped over the threshold and looked around. Worn black leather couch, guitar hanging off a hook on the wall, and several other guitars hiding in various cases scattered about. A grubby galley kitchen sat to their left, though it wasn't dirty, just well-used. It was actually in use at that very moment.

A pot boiled up with some sort of red sauce and Nico hurried over, turning down the burner and giving the sauce a quick stir. This snapped Carla to attention; she was in the home of a stranger she'd met in a bar, prepared to eat food he was preparing wearing her emergency underwear. What was she doing? To be fair, she figured people did a lot more than eat food and wear underwear with strangers they met online. How bad could this be?

"All right," he said, giving his red sauce one last stir. "I hope you like meatballs."

"You have no idea," Carla said, thinking back to the meal she had just consumed a few hours ago.

"Huh? Oh, cool." Nico said. He lifted the pot to a different burner and grabbed some bowls. "Want a drink? If I remember correctly, you were a gin kind of lady."

Carla couldn't help but laugh. Of course he knew that—how could anyone in the greater Cambridge/Boston area not notice that? Every sip of alcohol tended to raise her voice a decibel. "If *I* remember correctly, I said I was a clear alcohols lady, but who knows, maybe tonight I'm more of a beer lady."

"Fair enough," Nico chuckled, dimples coming out to play again as he grinned. "Stout okay?"

"Totally," Carla agreed even though it wasn't. It was a thousand degrees out—who drank stout in the summer? Nico, apparently. She'd forced herself to grow accustomed to IPAs so as not to rely entirely on lagers that were so light they may as well be whipped, but a stout? Flavorless and with the consistency of molasses. It was hard on a steaming day, but she didn't want to be difficult.

He cracked the cap off and the bottle hissed at the heat for a minute before the deep brown liquid was poured into a glass. He extracted a separate glass bottle sporting a Maker's Mark label from the cabinet and poured some amber fluid into a tumbler. She grabbed their drinks and walked to his couch, placing them on the table that sat in front of it. Ha! It was particle board furniture. She felt slightly more comfortable knowing that something in this apartment was clearly from IKEA.

Nico joined her on the couch with two bowls and set them down. Carla looked at the bowl, full to the brim and piping hot. This was it. Her Everest. She could never not eat food; instinct would kick in and she'd force it down if she had to. Surely there was nothing more rude than failing to finish a meal someone had made for you.

"So," Nico started, sipping his whiskey.

"So, what?"

"Tell me anything about yourself."

"Well…" Shit. What was she supposed to say? It was like a test. The worst test ever. "I'm a debt collector." Starting off with a bang.

"You're The Man."

"Correction, I'm The *Wo*man," Carla added snidely.

"Okay, okay," Nico conceded. "Why?"

"Why what?"

"Why a debt collector?"

"Oh! Well, I was in college," she began, sipping her beer. Carla had a theory that alcohol disintegrated food. The more alcohol she could dump into her body, the more likely she would be able to scarf down the meatballs. "But as I slowly watched money I didn't have fly away, I thought what would be more fun than being broke would be *not* being broke. So, I stopped."

She determinately bit into a meatball.

"You stopped what?"

"Going to school," Carla clarified, taking another swig of beer. She looked wistfully at the guitars in the corner. "I was actually at—"

"To become a debt collector?"

Nico's interruption caught her off guard and she continued, "Yeah. I figured that collecting student debt or any debt really seemed like a thriving market. So, rather than get chased, I'd be the chaser."

Carla was free and clear by this point too. Earlier in her career, aggressively calling people and banging down doors didn't seem like the chore it was these days. Paying off one year of school had flown by quicker than anticipated. But, without the need to pay off her bills, she had let her attention slide elsewhere—a song, a guy, a drink with friends here and there.

"Makes sense."

"Tell me something about you," Carla said. She wanted to turn the attention elsewhere while she polished off her second dinner.

"Well, I was born in San Diego."

"Really? That's awesome. California looks like a dream."

Nico's features twisted in disappointment. "It's so basic. I wanted to escape the minute I could look around and actually see stuff. I wanted to be near things that were real. You know?"

"I wouldn't want to be near bullshit all day."

"Exactly!" So, I came here for school and you know… that ended. So, I figured it needed to restart," he recalled with a laugh. "Plus, that way the bills are being paid by someone else." He emptied out his whiskey and went to pour some more. As he did, Carla shoved another meatball in her mouth, thankful he'd only given her two and caught a glimpse of something else that interested her.

"What's that?"

"What's what?"

"On the back of your arm. The tattoo."

"My boat."

"Of course you have a boat," she muttered. His family must be loaded. What normal guy in their mid-twenties studying music in grad school could afford a leather couch in a one-bedroom apartment in Davis Square?

"No! Not literally. I mean, I wish it was actually my boat. I just mean, I don't feel at all settled. Maybe when I do, I'll add an anchor."

"I get that."

"Yeah?"

"Yeah, I'm latched into life here. All the pieces exist, but I can't make them fit. I just don't feel quite right."

He nodded. "This is your California."

She couldn't understand his dissonance for California. It was a big state. Still, they had established something was calling to them and it wasn't waiting for them at home. Carla, feeling triumphant at reaching the summit of mount meatball, washed the food down with the rest of her beer, which Nico then quickly replaced.

They talked for hours, or at least until the sun disappeared. The time came when Carla felt vindicated in her last-minute undergarment change as she and Nico slowly leaned toward each other. Their faces didn't fit together perfectly—in fact, Carla quasi-smashed her face into his. It was a miracle she didn't bruise herself, but grace had really never been her strong suit. They got up, faces still attached to one another, and while he took strong purposeful steps to his room, she ambled along, clumsily planting one foot behind the other. Once they made it the actual bed, the choreography didn't much improve—well, not on her end. Her stomach was also pretty full considering she'd just scarfed down two dinners and three beers—not optimal for high intensity activity—but she was trying to make due with what she had. Unfortunately, what she had was all the grace of a corgi on roller skates. At any rate, they arrived at their destination.

If time had flown by when they were talking, a concord had brought them straight into morning. As she laid there with blue-grey light invading Nico's room, Carla realized it wasn't going to be a productive day at work by any means. She wanted to sleep, but her body was still buzzing.

MY TYPE

"Well, well, look who dropped off the map."

"Oh stop."

"No ma'm, I cannot." Jas leaned backward into his apartment, clearing the doorway for Carla to freely pass through. She sauntered across their living room and found her usual spot on their couch.

"Do you have any pizza? I'm hungry."

"So you barge into our home after over a week of nothing and demand pizza?"

"You heard me correctly."

"And I'm supposed to just reward this complete absence and lack of apology with food?"

"I was hoping so."

"Well, all right." He grabbed one of the boxes that sat on the kitchen peninsula. "But Summer's not home yet, so leave the mushroom slices in there for her."

"Yavolt!"

Jas collapsed on the other end of the couch. "Actually," he grabbed the other pepperoni, non-mushroom slice that remained after Carla had taken hers.

"So what's up?" Carla bit the pizza and savored the grease and spice of the pepperoni.

"You know, same old, same old." He shrugged. "Guitar Center is treating me fine as always."

"Cool. Why's Summer so late? It's like nine."

"She probably stayed to try and convince her mom about the coffee thing."

"Oh, why doesn't she just do it?"

"What do you mean *just do it?*"

"Why doesn't she just set up a table and chairs and keep some coffee going in a coffee maker with some muffins in the back?"

"I don't think that's really what she had in mind to make it work."

"But she could point at it and be all like *hey, look I sold some stuff, it works.*"

"That isn't how that stuff goes. It's more of a revamp type of situation. She has a whole plan. A good one. But she probably needs a real investment into it from her mom or a business loan."

"Seems risky."

"If you don't make some moves every now and then, nothing bad ever happens, but nothing good does either."

"Well," Carla said through a mouth of pizza, "I don't know much, but I do know that loans are the devil."

Jas laughed. "We aren't like your loan people! This is necessary. Like for a future."

"That's what the guy buying a kitty wheelchair said a week ago."

The front door abruptly swung open. "I can't handle this day any more." Summer slumped into the kitchen and dropped her bag at the base of the counter.

"No go with your mom?" Carla piped up, causing Summer's head to whip around.

"Oh my God," she clutched her chest, feigning a heart attack. "It's the magical vanishing woman."

"Well, see now, you're *both* just being dramatic."

"Oh please." Summer threw some slices of pizza onto a plate. "I've seen you practically every other day since we were, like, seven or whatever."

"So what's up with operation coffee shop?"

"Don't change the subject."

"Personally, I don't see why you don't just throw out some stale muffins and call it a day."

"Because old people are old and they're set in their ways, even if their book store hasn't turned a profit in over a year. There, so let's hear about your week now."

"No!"

"Get over it and spill. We assume early-century douche actually called you."

Carla sighed, "Yeah, Nico called me. He called me right after Sunday dinner."

"Ohhh."

"What? Stop that."

"No," Jas protested, "the last dude we had to listen to you go on and on about was frickin' Paul. We finally have a new one and we can't let the opportunity pass."

"Yuck." Summer was positioned on a chair to the side and was greedily eating pizza. "Like, why would you even date a guy named Paul to begin with?"

"I don't think the name Paul was the worst thing about him," Jas interjected.

"At any rate, a Paul, just seems so… stiff?"

"Sure you don't want to rephrase that one?"

"Anyway! How was Nico?"

"Again, phrasing."

"Oh my God, you get the point," Summer was getting exasperated. "What's up with that?"

"It's good."

"What do you mean good? Just good?"

"What's wrong with just good?"

"Do either of you want a beer?" Jas stood up.

"Yes," they said in unison.

"There's nothing wrong with good."

"There's nothing too great about good either."

Jas cracked three beers in the kitchen. "Usually when someone disappears for a week, there's more gushing. Summer's just looking for some juice."

"Ha ha," Summer grabbed a beer from his hand. Carla took the other.

"It was good," she'd done it and said it again. "After he called I wore the emergency underwear."

"Imma need you to back up a little bit. It just feels like there were a few pieces missing in there."

"Oh! Sorry, he called to invite me over for dinner and I didn't really know what that meant, so just to be safe rather than sorry, I figured that I'd wear the emergency underwear."

"I will assume it's a good thing you did that?"

"Sure was."

"So…" Summer slugged her beer and raised her eyebrows expectantly.

"He made a decent meatball."

"Did you eat all the meatballs?"

"Yep, and then I had seconds."

"Nice."

"You guys are special." Jas' attention returned to the television.

"What else did you do?"

"Uhh we mostly cooked and ate meatballs, watched TV. You know, that kinda stuff."

"So you like him?"

"I think it's casual?"

"You asked that though."

"Asked what?"

"Do you want to keep it casual or not?"

"I don't know, I'm just trying to have fun, and like, enjoy it all and stuff. Maybe just see what happens."

Summer leaned back in her chair. "Hear that,

Jas?"

"I did hear that, Summer."

"She wants to see where it goes."

"What's wrong with that?"

"Whenever we watch people see where it goes, it goes down in flames."

"You two saw where it went! It went into a marriage! And you moved in with each other crazy quick! Like four months."

"Isolated incident! Rarely happens. And, for the record, we decided to just be together forever. The government lured us into marriage with tax incentives."

"Just let her do her thing, Summer."

"Yeah, Summer, just let me do my thing. Maybe I just wanna have fun."

"Every time you just wanna have fun, you wind up having no fun."

"Sorry, I can't recall, might I be speaking to Josie at the moment?"

Summer's lip curled, "Buh, I feel like we're done here."

"Phew. Thank God."

"But just don't just do the sex with him. Like, make him take you out or something."

"Who cares if we just do the sex? I'm just having fun."

"You said it again."

"That I'm just having fun? I'm young! I'm allowed to screw around. You guys, also are the last people on earth to talk."

This made Jas' ears perk up, "How so?"

"Oh please," Carla snorted, "When you two first got together all I heard wa-"

She couldn't finish her sentence as Summer essentially vaulted over to the couch where Carla sat. "Don't!" she yelped as Jas erupted with laughter.

"Summer, there's a reason you weren't ever

recruited for the CIA. You think that surprises me at this point?" Jas had a true smile that cracked through his entire face. Giddily and heartily, he could pump out chuckles. They were warm in tone.

"Summer, Summer," Carla dodged her, "there should be nothing about this as a surprise here."

"About what?" She gave up and rolled onto her side, having now displaced Carla.

"About me just always wanting to have fun. Sex is always there. It's everywhere."

"How so?"

"It's just everywhere I go and same for you! I don't mean how you made me sit through sessions on sessions of you going on non-stop about Jas'-"

"Yes, stop now!"

"Whatever, anyway, all I'm saying is that it's in our television and on the street. Oh! And, the music! That's everywhere."

"Not getting your point."

"My point is, there's nothing wrong with a little," Carla threw a few hip thrusts out there for emphasis. "It's everywhere, it's great. Josie liked it so much she got knocked up before walking down the aisle."

"I'm not saying it isn't everywhere or that it's bad. No Catholic guilt bullshit here." She held up her hands. "I'm just saying you don't seem so happy every time a Paul situation waltzes on in and you tend to date a lot of Pauls, if I say so."

"I hear what you're saying."

"Thank you."

"I'm still gonna keep seeing him."

"I didn't tell you not to. I'm just telling you, try dating him rather than playing it cool."

"I'm just gonna see what happens. He's way more my type than Paul ever was anyway."

"Paul is your type, and they're all Pauls."

"What about the original Paul?"

"Patient Zero? Who's that?"

"Ugh, none other than your big bro. Duh."

"Oh." Summer readjusted her position again so as to sit more comfortably.

Jas' attention was finally caught and he looked up and around at the mention of Arlo. "I mean, I'm not totally sure what a Paul is, but why is Arlo a Paul?"

"Because he was once such a Paul."

Carla, tired of standing, claimed Summer's old chair. "High school Arlo was grown-up Paul."

"So Arlo used to be a total dick?"

"Yeuh!" Summer shot out at him. "Well, not a huge dick, but he definitely slept with everyone on earth… Who went to Cambridge High and then just threw them aside without a second glance."

"No, Sir. He lives out in California now and he's all settled in with Dylan!"

"Yeah, now he is. Wasn't always like that."

"Dude," Carla was distracted, "how sick must California be right now?"

Jas didn't care, he was on guard, "I've never known him as anything other than a sweet dude."

"Well," Summer said, "You didn't know him when we were about thirteen." She gestured impressively between herself and Carla, waiting for her to jump in. "Carla!"

Carla jumped out of the sand dune of daydream she'd diverted into. She bet Arlo was sitting on a sand dune right now, maybe. Probably. "Ah, that would be a yes. I'm assuming you're talking about…"

"Yeuh!"

"Yeah."

"Do I get to know what yeah means?" Jas getting impatient.

Carla smiled as they started to travel back in time. "So you have to get, Jas, that when Josie wasn't around to torture, Arlo was our back up plan."

"Shocking."

As Summer started into the tale for Jas, Carla smiled slightly, letting the sound of rough garage rock flood forward from her memory. It had been snowing that day and Carla and Summer were seeking shelter inside from blustery winds. They tracked extra snow inside Carla's house first, but her mother quickly tried to shoo them upstairs so as to not leave a huge pile of wet sloppy dirt in the kitchen in time to annoy her father. They knew Josie was out that day, so they were drawn to the warm din of Summer's home. Summer's parents were more frequently absent, and Arlo would be there to antagonize. After they had kicked off their boots near the door and helped themselves to the complete store of Wonderballs that remained in Summer's kitchen, it was time to meander down the hall to where Arlo's little hovel was.

It was the fuzzy twang of the guitar strums on The Undertones' "Teenage Kicks" that had caught their attention far sooner than it otherwise would have been though. Drumbeats rolled down the carpeted hallway, growing louder as they took each step. They pressed their small feet into the fluff of worn pink shag, and as they slowly reached their destination, they heard a voice, though not of the lead singer, but of a girl.

"That's not my mom," Summer whispered. The two looked at each other and grinned.

"Does Arlo have a, a *girlfriend?*"

Summer giggled, "Nope."

"Should we scare them?"

"Yup."

"Maybe we should leave them alone?"

"Definitely not." Summer continued to whisper. "Plus, my mom would get pissed. Maybe we can blackmail him into getting us extra gushers or something."

"Cool."

"I don't think that's right?" the sound came as a muffle from behind the door through the hollow sound of rock. A girl's voice.

"It's definitely right." That one was Arlo.

"What do you think it is?" Carla asked. The two girls pressed their ears up to the door.

"Oh. Okay." They could hear.

"Good?"

"Yeah, it's good."

"I don't get it," Summer said, "I'm having trouble hearing through the music." They both attempted to shove their ears up against the door firmly, but it was more than they bargained for. The door wasn't closed tight, so Arlo would also end up with more than he bargained for; the two preteens went down with a crash into the room, which contained Arlo and a very confused blonde girl who was largely hidden behind him. Of what poked out of the covers, she seemed to come to what was going on a little quicker and then screamed aloud, "Oh my God!"

"Oh my God!" announced Summer.

Arlo flopped out of the bed like a dead fish desperately grabbing at a spare blanket to hide behind while his companion had fully sunk under all remaining covers at that point. "Summer, get the fuck out!"

"I, ugh, I, fuck!" was all Carla could manage.

Summer grabbed Carla's hand and the two ran out, all the while, Summer screaming, "You better get us Fruit by the Foot or I'm telling Mom and Dad!"

The two girls booked it back to the door and pulled their boots back on; they grabbed their jackets, too but it was paramount they make it back to Carla's. They arrived as Ana had finished cleaning up their last mess. "Oh no! Boots off now. I'm not doing this twice. If your father had happened to see this he would've had a coronary."

"Okay, sure!" They disrobed in the doorway area

in record time and then scurried upstairs.

"Wait!" Ana yelled after them, "Why weren't you two wearing your jackets? You'll catch your death that way!" They'd already made it into Carla's room, her mother standing at the bottom of the stairs talking to no one. "Isn't anyone hungry?"

"No, Mom!" Carla shut the door and looked at Summer. They erupted into laughter.

"I wonder if he'll actually give us the Fruit by the Foot," Summer pondered aloud after a beat.

Fruit by the Foot was not what Carla had particularly taken from the afternoon. Gushers and Wonderballs and Fruit by the Foot had officially been pushed onto the back burner after that day. There were more interesting things to think about and wonder about. It also still took her a full six months before she could look Arlo in the eye again.

Carla's memory was winding down, as was Summer's retelling of the story, "…And that bastard never even got me my Fruit by the Foot. Fruit by the Feet?"

"I think foot is fine?"

"Well, that was a riveting tale," Jas said, "not sure that makes Arlo a Paul though."

"That's because I'm not done yet. That girl's name was Jenny."

"Okay."

"And do you know how much we saw Jenny after that?" Carla asked.

"I have no idea."

"The answer is never again! Because after that there was Sarah, and then Maria, and then Alexa, and so on and so forth!"

"That's not totally true, Summer," Carla interjected.

"How so?"

"Don't you remember? Jenny did show up again, it was just to curse out Arlo after he didn't bother talking to her anymore because of Sarah."

"Oh, yeah, fair point."

"So you're telling me, my boy Arlo, is kind of a-"

"Fuckboy."

"Oh."

"Yeah, *oh*."

"But, not forever! Just a while."

"Isn't that called being in high school?" Jas interjected on the absent Arlo's behalf?"

"You trying to tell me something about your high school days, my friend?"

"I don't recall you being a saint…"

The three fell into silence, leaving Carla to her own thoughts once again. "I think this is where I will be taking off."

Summer curled her lip under in a mock sad face.

"I have debt to collect in the morning."

"Ever get that guy with the kitty wheelchair?"

Carla's shoulder's slumped, "Alas, I didn't." She stood up and looped her bag around her shoulder. She was tired all of a sudden, and the thoughts of Arlo through the years were swirling through her head. She walked to the door and Jas followed her.

"Well, hopefully we see you again before the week is out, but just in case, have a good one."

"Oh, shut up, I'll see you again."

"Hey, just saying. Go have yourself some fun."

After Carla walked out the door, she heard the bolt click into place behind her. The walk home was short anyway, but as thoughts of Arlo growing into the kind and patient adult he was today and his Southern California home and her own romantic entanglements floated through her brain, it was as though she had teleported back to her doorstep. She skipped the broken step despite it being dark and arrived in her tiny apartment. It was lights out, no wind-down required.

The morning air was still cool as the sun had risen only recently and had not yet had time boil the earth. Capitalizing on this uncharacteristically crisp morning, Carla chose to walk her way to work. The bridge was easily the best part of the walk. It was a place to greet the sun in the morning, drink in Boston's skyline, and watch people trying to learn to sail capsize. It offered a plethora of benefits at any rate, and today she went with the former as only the beginnings of sunbeams shot a warm glow across the universe. It certainly wasn't a time efficient method for her to get to work, but it was for that reason that Carla frequently chose this route. The ferocity she had once brought to her job upon arrival had dwindled not long after she'd repaid her loan, a paltry sum when compared to the people she knew who had opted for the full boat and emerged with an actual degree, but still a fair chunk of change. She had felt good then. She had accomplished something that so few her age did.

Upon her arrival at work, she set the coffee cup she'd filled in the break room down on her otherwise barren desk, save a desktop setup and telephone. It was hard to think of putting up any photos or decorations. She could leave at any given moment after all, so what would be the point in spreading herself all over the place? The warm glow she had felt upon paying her loan off had long left, and the empty abyss of going to the same job every day that she didn't feel particularly passionate about was what currently lay before her. She felt certain that bringing in a few family photos and making her desk a home would seal her fate into the gray flannel life.

She could try cat guy again, or she could brush it off to the side. It didn't feel like an enormous deal. Plus, she had a second skip on her plate as well. Greta Winchendon. Why oh why did Greta Winchendon not pay her bills? Also, who the hell was named Greta?

As it turned out, an aging woman with a seemingly limited amount of patience. "Hello?" Her sleepy, croaky voice answered the phone.

"Hello mam, I'm callin-"

"Hello?!" The woman's voice suddenly jumped several octaves and decibels.

"Hello, Ms. Greta Winchendon?"

A piercing whine sliced into Carla's eardrums. "This is she. Who is this?" the voice on the other end of line demanded.

"Well, I'm calling on behalf of-"

"Is this about my Elemis?"

"Sorry?"

"My Elemis, I put the order in seemingly weeks ago. I called the number so I could get the special price."

"No, actually this is in regards to-"

"It comes with collagen in it. You wouldn't understand, you sound young. But let me tell you what a lifetime of summers down The Cape can do to a person's skin."

"Right, of course," this call was going even worse than average.

"Oh, it must've been at least a week."

"Mam, I need to follow up with you on several missed payments."

"What?!" The idle tone of a lonely woman suddenly whipped into a state of ferocity.

"On your credit cards, mam, you've missed multiple payments and we need to-"

"You are calling up a woman of an advanced age to try and grease her down for money? For shame!"

This was it, the moment when she would indeed stick to her guns. "Mam, it's hardly shameful to recoup the money that's ow-"

"I won't hear of it!" Greta interrupted her yet again. Apparently, Greta wouldn't hear of anything. "I just finished telling you about the collagen and the summers down the Cape."

Carla thought vaguely of following her sister up to the Revere strip every summer and watching her rub oil all over her skin. Not only did it fail to repel the sun's damaging rays, it invited them. Greta seemed to have followed a similar routine for triple the amount of time. Josie would regularly fight the crisping edges of her skin. "You could try coco butter; my sister uses it. Says it moisturizes pretty well." Shit. She'd done it again.

"Cocoa butter? You are young. Honey, wait a few years and you'll learn that all the cocoa butter and aloe infused moisturizer won't get you anywhere."

Carla would've put money on the fact that Greta most likely had skin akin to an under-basted, over roasted Thanksgiving turkey, and that no amount of collagen in the world could have solved that by this point her life. "At any rate, mam-"

"Oh, don't you fuss at me, young lady! Now I can't be on the phone all day with you. There's a Lock and Lock set of glass bowls and I need to call in and snatch them up."

"Should you really b-" but it didn't matter, even when Greta Winchendon wasn't speaking, she managed to cut Carla off.

Carla set the phone back in its receiver and stared at it. Another skip untraced. It was her other phone that had now come alive with buzzing, distracting her from the elderly woman with a bad QVC habit.

There was instead a far more interesting young man with a bass guitar and what felt like twenty fingers texting her. A man that made albeit subpar meatballs, but satisfying enough, nonetheless.

Would she be around later? Well, based on the fact that Mrs. Winchendon had given her the shaft, tomorrow would always exist for badgering more delusional cat owners and old people, and it was a beautiful day outside; yes, she would be around.

The minutes ticked by, and she murdered each one waiting for the time she could finally leave and go hang out with him again. She was doing research, she was sitting on her phone in the bathroom laughing at whatever Facebook video Nico had tagged her in, she doodled on some paper and looked at how much area rugs cost on Amazon.

Her phone buzzed once more as she stood by the coffee machine and she refilled her cup for the umpteenth time. She kept a careful eye out for Arthur. But, when Carla read the text, she was left disappointed. No Nico. He had a last minute rehearsal come up; could they see each other another time? Yeah, obviously they could.

Carla leaned back in her chair, tossed her phone on her desk and stared at it for a minute. She glanced to the landline, equally disappointed. Thus far, it had been a no win day. Her coffee cup remained full enough for a few slugs, but she vaulted herself off her chair anyway and grabbed the cup.

Sauntering into the lounge area for the second time that day, she dumped the remaining lukewarm liquid into the sink and threw the mug under the Keurig spout. Water went in the back and a pod was deployed into the top bit of the machine. She stared entranced as the mug slowly filled up with dark roast.

"Tough day?" Tim, her coworker, asked from the door.

"More like a bad year." She straightened up and spun around. "How's life in accounting treating you?"

"Oh, it's a non-stop party." He smiled and rolled up his sleeves.

"Wanna swap parties? You can try greasing an old lady down for the all money she's been dumping into rejuvenating facial creams, hideous handbags, and eighty different kinds of vases."

"A tempting offer."

"I mean who even wants those vases? And who even wants flowers in their home?"

"Uhm, a lot of people?"

"All that means is that a lot of people like dead, decrepit petals making a mess everywhere in their houses."

"Can't say I ever thought about it like that." He walked to the Keurig and removed Carla's now full cup and set his own down in place. "What I'm more wondering about is why an old person needs rejuvenating facial creams."

"Thank. You. What is with that? You're old. Time to throw in the towel, Grandma!"

As the Keurig farted out the last sputters of coffee, the two coworkers descended into chuckles. "I think this is what happens when you're stuck under florescent lighting for too long."

"It's probably a conspiracy. It's probably in every office building and that's how they control our minds. Maybe the coffee's even spiked too."

"You really got your tinfoil hat on today."

"The Man is trying to keep us down."

"We are the Man."

Carla raised her eyebrows and mockingly lowered her voice, "That's how they get you the most; they're making us think we're the Man."

"You've really been having yourself a day, huh?"

"Dude, I really have."

"Why don't you just knock off early? I doubt Arthur'd even notice. Hell, half the time he's leaving early to go to the doctor's for one thing or another."

"I know, right?"

"I just want to shake him and scream, 'It's a

deviated septum!'"

"I did just pour this coffee though."

Tim shrugged. "I gotta get back anyway, I have a computer screen I need to stare blankly at."

She laughed once more, "I'll see you." They both grabbed their cups and walked their separate ways.

Carla stared at her own screen some more and considered what Tim had said. There wasn't any point in staying much more that day; she may as well take off. Considering her blank-screened phone once more, she told herself the only downside to the recent turn of events was that she wouldn't be getting laid, but the upside was that she could just chill out and have a minute to herself. She chipped away at her nails and took one more sip of coffee before thinking better of the agita that was probably brewing away.

Carla had walked to work. She slept better at night with a walk, and while she had done her walking in the morning that particular day, it no longer felt like enough. Sitting all day was tiring enough; living through her own feelings had really worn her out after that. The trains were too packed and the people too angry. The sun felt so hot, even so late in the day that she could feel the sweat evaporate off her brow, but through mental exhaustion, she was still on the brink of physically jumping out of her skin.

She set her course to take her over the Longfellow Bridge with the possibility of an eventual detour to the bookstore. She took a peek over the edge, hoping for a capsize, but there were none to be had that day. Only highly competent sailing trainees and a duck boat full of tourists. She wished that anything these days filled her with the undulated joy that a duck boat tour brought to a tourist.

What occurred to her as she reached the other side of the bridge was that maybe she needed to just focus on lyrics for a while. All she did was sit and strum and while she strung together some reasonable sounding melodies, they all had downward arpeggios and chords that belonged in bottoming out refrains. She needed the warmth of a G or the light airiness of D, but she grasped at nothing. It would maybe be the words she could start with and then she wouldn't be begging for those happier tones. Summer had been thick with a heavy atmosphere so far, but her heartbeat was far more rapid-fire than it had been in months.

She curved her route off the main road, avoiding the mess of students and commuters and wound her way through the back streets to the bookstore once again. Summer sat at the back of the house as usual. Her laptop was open and she was squinting at the screen, scrunching her eyebrows to the point where a vertical line sat between them.

"Well, don't hurt yourself."

Summer raised up a middle finger at Carla as she continued to look at the screen.

"Now, that's not very nice. Terrible customer service."

"I'm trying," Summer looked up, "to figure out what the hell goes in a business plan."

"Why?"

"I want to make this into more of a coffee shop."

"I thought that was operation brew-some-coffee-behind-the-counter-and-throw-some-stale-muffins-from-BJ's-at-the-customers?"

"It was, but then I realized I was serious. I don't want to half ass this."

"Oh. So what goes into a business plan?"

"Statistics."

"Do you have those?"

"Nope."

"How do you get them?"

Summer leaned back with her mouth contorted into a look of distaste. "The hell if I know. I don't even know why I sit here all day every day."

Carla felt highly suspicious that this little piece of real estate could yield anything, but it seemed cruel to dump that load of bricks on Summer, so out of pity she played along. "What else do you put in a business plan? I guess what you plan on doing to make money?"

"Yeah, I mean it's pretty self-explanatory."

"How could you make money other than on coffee and yuppie pastries?"

"Sell books?"

"Oh."

"Yeah." Summer's eyes jumped up and down on her face in a jerky motion, "Exactly."

"Well, who could you sell them to?"

"I feel like you're starting from square one here."

"I realized on my walk here today that I needed to do that with my songs because it's been forever since I've made one worth listening to."

"So, what's square one for you?"

"Starting with the words. So," Carla tried to steer the conversation back to Summer, "who is gonna buy your books and eventually, your crappy coffee?"

"No one around here reads."

"That's bullshit."

"No, it isn't!"

"Yeah it is, people who can't find apartments close to the T keep moving farther and farther into our turf. At this point we basically can't even afford to rent in our turf."

"So, your coworkers, is what you're saying?"

"Yeah, and like, what about all the schools?"

"So your coworkers and former classmates?"

"If you can't exploit those closest to you, who can you exploit? It's basically the American dream."

"Right."

"When I was at school, we had a bookstore we were supposed to buy from, but I had this one professor who wasn't about supporting big corporations or something, even though one was currently sending him his paychecks. Anyway, what I'm saying is…"

"What are you saying?"

"Don't Greta me!"

"What?"

"I mean, ugh. Anyway, he would send us to some beaten, off-the-path bookstore to buy our books. So, probably there are a bunch of other profs out there like that one."

"Why would students order their books through me?"

"Because their professor won't refer them to the bookstore, they'll tell them they have to buy it from you. It's a whole thing."

"It seems fishy."

"It's something."

"Why can't you just do that for you?"

"How so?"

"You sat there and just pulled something out like it was nothing. Just do that but with a song."

"It isn't that easy though."

"Why?"

"You should know why for yourself! When it's your baby it's harder. Coming up with something you don't care about… You can just spew that out." Carla hastily added, "Not that I don't care about you."

"Fine, yeah."

"I just need to try something else, I think." She looked wistful.

"Something else how?"

"I want to try something happy."

Summer feigned shock, leaning back and clutching her chest and a most dramatic display.

"Hah, hah. I'm dying with laughter here."

"You need to stop writing about Paul."

"They aren't all about Paul."

"…and Ioen."

"He was just a fuckboy."

Summer sat straight up and clasped her hands together, further mocking Carla, "Oh, but Summer, he *cooks* for me and he's *traveled* all over the *world*." She nearly fell over laughing at her own joke.

"Okay, he was a fuckboy with a cute accent."

"They both were, Paul just had a better routine down. Plus, he looked good on paper to mom and dad. You know, that's one of the ways they get you."

"He always had one foot in my circle and one out. Do you think it would've been like that if he hadn't been friends with Josie and Nick?"

"Who knows? He looked good on paper to you; you probably looked that way to him too."

"We sucked though, didn't we?"

"Pretty much."

Carla leaned forward onto the counter, listening to Ingrid Michaelson echo out of Summer's computer. The words from "Empty Bottle" floated past her, a hollow reminder that blasted her back to Summer and Jas' couch years ago.

She had been tapping her fingers to a gentle snare then as well, though she continually tapped her knee. "It's been a full week," she'd said, confused.

"Take me through it," Jas said.

Summer spoke up, "Well, to be fair, I told her to message him."

"Did you?"

"Yeah, I figured he's always the one doing it. Maybe I was supposed to do it instead."

"Did he ever answer after that?"

"Yeah, he was nice. We went back and forth a couple times."

"But you didn't hang out after that or anything?"

"No, but I know he works with Nick and I figured that since Nick was really busy with work that week that maybe he was too."

"Don't they work in construction?"

"Yeah," Carla said. "So what?"

"I don't think Nick's been having a busy week." Summer punched him covertly from the side. "It just isn't really a thing. I doubt they were getting overtime."

"Well, then where else would Nick have been? Josie's said he's been having a busy phase at work."

"I think with guys, Carla," Jas was trying to be nice clearly, "if they want to see you they see you."

"Do you think I'm gonna see him again?"

"The likelihood of that is getting lower with each passing day."

"Well, why doesn't he just say that?"

"Say what?"

"That he's not up for anything?"

Summer shrugged. "Honestly, I think it's just easier not to."

"So we're done? Just like that? I have to just fit together puzzle pieces?"

"Sorry, dude."

Carla looked down at her phone as though this inanimate object had let her down rather than the person on the other end of the line. "I don't get it though. We had fun the last time we hung out! I stayed at his place."

Summer sat up on the couch and angled her body to face Carla, bracing herself to deliver an unfortunate piece of information. "He's probably found someone else to stay at his place."

"Is he an idiot?"

"Yeah," Jas said, "he's friends with Nick; we were

pretty sure that would tell you all you needed to know, but I guess not."

"But his best friends are my brother-in-law and sister. We're gonna run into each other for the rest of our lives."

"Based on this conversation, I think that's gonna bother you more than him."

Carla sat back and grabbed her beer. A week ago, she'd reached the six-month mark of sleeping next to the same person nearly every night and here she was now, having to recalibrate herself to being the bigger person for the foreseeable future. She wanted to tell Josie to excommunicate him, but she'd seen enough nineties rom-coms to know what that looked like. She was relegated to anticipating reactions and feelings, she'd roll her eyes when needed, brush it off, or act like she hadn't noticed. To do otherwise would be a point of notable embarrassment for her. Carla had allowed someone to hurt her feelings, not cool. How dare she make such a misstep? So if Josie were to mention him or bring him around, it was clear that her role in all this was to smile and brush it off and not care. No labels, just fun, and that's what she'd meant to be doing through the entire stint of whatever they'd been doing. There was no time to practice like the present, in fact, so after Carla had taken another swig of beer, choking back over-carbonated alcohol along with her feelings and merely offered, "Paul's a dick, whatever." And with a shrug, she put the messy ordeal of having emotions behind her and centered her thoughts on Ingrid Michaelson.

Or was that Ingrid in the present? Her memories bled back into reality and she realized that Summer had refocused on her laptop screen once again. It was probably just a futile plan anyway, trying to turn the bookstore into a coffee shop. But, Summer seemed so focused, Carla didn't want to blow the wind out of her sails. Plus, she could understand dreams; unfortunately she could also understand probability. The sun had continued to wane outside and she was now in no mood to be alone. Her plans, however brief, had fallen through, so just as she had when they were kids, she implored Summer to play with her.

"Summer."

"Yes?"

"Pay attention to me."

Summer looked up at her. "Hi Carla!"

"Wanna go do something?"

"I mean I would, but I simply cannot keep up with the masses teeming to get in here," Summer said to an empty store.

"Wanna go get a drink?"

"Purple Salmon?"

"We may as well. If you don't mind."

"Naw, I don't care. It was an especially busy day, five whole people came in to buy stuff."

"Sick."

"Maybe for just a beer though; I didn't really hang out with Jas much the last two days between our working and his band-ing."

"That's fine by me; I just can't figure out what I want today." Carla didn't tell Summer the whole ordeal with Greta, or her up and down plans with Nico. She wasn't in the mood to demonstrate her ineptitude at work nor her disappointment at not seeing someone she was supposed to not care about seeing.

"Let me just go and grab my bag from the back."

Moments later, Summer returned and the two set off for the Purple Salmon. The momentary coolness of the bookstore was immediately replaced by the heat that was then trapped in her polyester skirt. Ballet flats completed an unobtrusive and horrifically uncomfortable look. That look that helped her fly under the radar so well at work would always make her stick out like a sore thumb in The Purple Salmon, a fact she was acutely aware of once more upon entrance into the bar.

Not long after Summer and Carla took their seats and ordered their drinks did Carla's phone go off. As Summer was distracted by a man attempting a rendition of *Cecilia* on a plastic pickle tub, Carla snuck a peek at her phone, Nico. He was able to hang out once again;a band mate fell through on him, so he called the whole thing off, stating he would much rather hang out with her.

It was at this point that Carla then looked up at Summer, confusion on her face as the pickle tub aficionado continued his tale of a broken heart and shaken confidence. How could she quickly dip out? Summer had gone out at her behest, and beyond that, jumping up to go hang out with someone the moment in which they beckoned you was a decidedly terrible look.

There was, however, the other end of this, Carla thought. It became awfully tiring to go running back and forth all over the place, withholding responses and sending the right words at the right time. It was all a game, but after you play the same game for too long, you know all the moves and it gets really boring. Maybe she didn't want to play the game. Maybe she just wanted to hang out with someone she happened to like… and could have really good orgasms with.

It was with that thought in mind that she responded to Nico, telling him she would make it as soon as she could. She just needed her out, and as the songs wore on with Pickle tub continuing his assault on the works of Paul Simon, she became antsier and antsier, wanting only to leave as quickly as she could. Suddenly and luckily, she found that a break point was approaching. Quite literally, it approached in the form of Jas. Relieved she would only kind of be ditching a friend rather than completely doing so, she smiled up at him as he lumbered closer to them from they door.

"Hey there." Jas sat down and gave Summer a quick kiss.

"Hey yourself, stranger," Summer responded, looking pretty pleased.

The two sat there next to each other, looking happy, with Jas' arm on the back of Summer's chair. They jig-sawed into each other perfectly. To Carla, it looked so nice, and yet, so unattainable.

"So, what're we drinking?"

"Well, it's Tuesday, so not much," Carla said.

"But it's my Friday!"

"Lucky you!"

Summer held up a hand for the waitress to swing by once more. "I'll grab another."

"I think I'm actually out." Carla produced several bills and threw them down on the table.

"What? I just got here!"

"Hang with your wifey. I had a long day at work."

Summer looked disappointed, "It's true. We said only a quick one."

"I'm just tired; sorry guys."

"I'm only messing with you."

"We need to hang out soon though," Summer insisted, "like for real for real."

"Definitely. I swear." Carla stood up and smoothed the polyester skirt down her legs, wishing she was wearing something else. Before exiting through the door, she glanced back with a small pang of guilt at the couple whose backs were facing her. Summer had leaned slightly into Jas in a motion of effortless comfort as the two were laughing about something. She turned and emerged into the soupy air for the final time that night and set off to Nico's, where maybe she could lean on him in the same way.

SOUNDCHECK

Nico's bed was lopsided. Upon her first arrival at his apartment, it had been squishy and comfortable. Carla had passed out, unaware, and woke up the next morning in a relaxed, well-rested state. As the months wore on, it became apparent to her that there was a problem with the bed. No matter how far to left she positioned her body, inevitably she would roll downhill to the right and eventually find herself midway through the night pressed up against him in an overly hot embrace. He had a summer's worth of hot air caught up in his room and it was stifling; the last thing either of them wanted was midnight snuggling.

On this particular morning, Carla once again woke up far too early, as Nico continued on in a deep state of slumber. She looked over, frustrated at him. He wasn't even that much larger than her, yet the bed happened to form a divot specifically to the shape of his body. So while he rested peacefully, she was climbing back up to the summit of the left-side of the mattress once more.

A cerulean blue had crept through the room, an

indication that it was certainly earlier than six, which was an indication that Carla would be arriving to work groggy. She looked over at Nico sleeping peacefully in the valley of his bed and resented him for it. With anyone else on earth, she would wake up for some fun before work. After trying this for the first time, she quickly learned it to be a mistake. While Carla didn't love her early mornings, Nico was completely incapable of tolerating them. He would get up for literally nothing. So, she laid there, as he had previously sent her a pining text when she had left without a trace.

Carla sat up on the back of her elbows and propped her body up against the headboard. Along the way, she tried to jostle the bed around as much as possible in a lame attempt of waking Nico out of his sleep. He wiggled around a bit, but ultimately landed in nearly the same position, only with his head facing her. She studied his features. Angular as they were, his jaw wasn't so roughly cut, and his lips were larger than average for a man, giving him a bit more softness. It was an odd in-between place they were occupying. Waking up and fleeing felt more like it was in her wheelhouse, but he didn't want that, or at least his text messages so indicated. No labels had been assigned either though, and she felt weary of pushing it.

She loudly cleared her throat a few times and finally found success. Nico blinked for a minute and she could see his eyes attempting to focus. She reached down and picked up her phone up off the floor. Ten of six. It wasn't as bad as she had thought. Nico reached an arm up and flopped it over her. "Is it that time already?"

"Nearly."

He hugged her legs. "That sucks."

Carla killed the alarm on her phone. Nothing was more grating than that of an alarm. It wasn't just a call to wake up, it was a nagging, incessant stab of a reminder. "You're telling me. I don't want to go to work."

Nico rolled back over on his back and looked up at the ceiling. "Yeah, that must suck."

Carla wanted to roll her eyes but managed suppress it. Even through her brief stint in college she had managed to hold down a job. Nico appeared to magically be able to just go to school and, well, that was about it. She kicked both her feet out from under the covers and angled her body out of bed. She needed to get home, shower and change before she went back into the office.

"You just gonna run out?"

"Yeah, I gotta kinda get going with my day, shower, coffee and all that." She picked up her pants off the ground and started to get dressed.

"Since I'm awake," he dramatically wrenched himself out of bed, "have some of my cold brew." He strode into his kitchen.

Carla hopped around in her bra trying to fit a leg into a pair of jeans and looked out. "It's okay, I can just grab something on the way."

"Yeah, you mean from a coffee shop?"

"Uh huh." She yanked a tank top over her head.

"I mean that's just another piece of plastic you're dumping into the environment."

It wasn't that Carla didn't care about sea turtles, it was that she didn't care about anything before seven in the morning. All she needed to do was drag her half asleep body into work so she could get her paycheck and survive. Telling that to someone whose personal duties in life presently included being a teaching assistant seemed like more of a mountain than she was willing to scale at the moment. "Right."

"I only drink my own cold brew. I make it in this." He extracted a glass carafe from his fridge. "It's from Japan."

"Cool." Carla stared at the black liquid. She wanted to be the person who brewed all her own cold coffee, but she was probably going to be the person who always bought her own coffee or pilfered it from work for free.

"You've really gotta make it yourself."

"Totally."

"There." He poured some into a carrier mug and added water. "So it isn't too strong for you."

"Thanks," she walked to him and took the mug. "I better get going." She kissed him, trying to hold her breath the whole time. She had no toothbrush there and feared her morning dragon breath.

"Why don't you just bring clothes here with you?"

It was the first time he suggested it to her. It felt good. She smiled, "Yeah, I guess I could do that."

"It just seems like it would save you time in the mornings. We wouldn't have to wake up so early."

"Yeah, next time. For sure." Carla picked up her purse from where she'd hurriedly dropped it on the floor the night before. She found her way back on the T and crammed her body up against angry morning commuters trying to the keep the travel mug upright, without dumping it everywhere. This is where a straw would've been ideal, though it did now stick in her mind that a straw would only further the current seagull genocide they were living through, so she supposed it was maybe just as well.

As she made her way home, she sipped the dark liquid. It was possibly one of the worst things she'd ever tasted. If this was the coffee heavily watered down, she was certain that either all homemade cold brew tasted like a foot or that his beans had gone bad. If that was even possible. She couldn't be sure. She tried one more sip, but the taste was so revolting she spat it out. So much for that. She dumped the rest into the grass outside her apartment and escaped upstairs. She practically ran out of her clothes through the shower and into some new attire. She looked at herself in the same old suffocating polyester pants, lycra blend button down and hard-soled ballet flats. The clothes were stiff and didn't sit on her body appropriately, making her look like a box. She hated her look a little more each day. Thirty minutes later, she found herself standing on the grey pavement outside of her grey office building about to walk into a grey day.

It was an administrative catch up day, Carla had told herself. Yet there she sat, with a pen and paper in front of her. She doodled away; there was a scribble here and there as well. The song she had so intently started months ago had fallen flat. Between work and Nico and trying to keep up with Summer and Jas so that she didn't appear to be neglecting anyone, she'd ultimately wound up neglecting her song.

It wasn't the same in another sense though. The happy, light, floating feeling that had once inhabited her not so long ago seemed to deflate slowly, and the words weren't flying out of her mind quite so easily these days. She wondered if it all possibly amounted to nothing more than sleep deprivation. It seemed though, that possibly the fire had died down a bit, and the shiny glow that had surrounded her when she had first met Nico was dimming a bit too. The words she managed to come up with felt slower and lower and she re-read them.

Sailing ships across the sea
I wondered where would they take me
I thought I'd found someone who could reflect

That was crap and she couldn't use it. There was no sense in trying to pump out anything more and she disgustedly dropped her pen on the drivel she'd just written.

"Hey."

Carla nearly fell out of her chair. The voice had come out of nowhere and cut through her thoughts.

Luckily, it was just Tim. "Jesus, you scared the crap out of me."

"Sorry! I actually meant to do just the opposite. I was by the Keurig again and I heard Arthur asking someone if they'd seen you in the office today."

"Damn."

"Yeah, I figured you might wanna know."

"Thanks, Tim" she placed an elbow over the notepad she had been scribbling on in an attempt to hide her true activities for the day thus far. She propped her head up in her hand.

It had been no use though. Tim had seen already, the lines were clearly arranged into stanzas, not bulleted notes. "Whatcha got there?"

"Ah, just some scribblings. It's my lunch." The lie flew from her mouth with ease.

"I don't care." He laughed and cocked his head. "Are you writing poetry or something?"

"No, it's just some lyrics to a song."

"Oh? You're a song writer?"

"Sometimes. Lately I've just been a debt collector." Actually, lately she'd just been having extended phone conversations with people who had overspent their money on items they didn't particularly need.

"I want to hear a song."

"I dropped out of Berkeley." The words defensively flew from her lips before she could even stop herself.

"Cool. I still want to hear a song. Write one and call it like, *The Tim Song*."

"So now I'm writing you a personal song? I should probably charge you."

"Don't send me to the poor house."

"I *am* pretty expensive."

"Well, let me know." He backed away, arms up.

She realized she was smiling to herself and relaxed into the back of her chair. The moment was brief though as she realized she was going to eventually have to speak with Arthur, and presumably about her lackluster performance. She went to swivel in her chair so she could face her desk, but it was useless as she found that Miriam was quickly approaching her and that was not good news.

Miriam could be described as average in every way except for one, that she held an administrative position under Arthur, and therefore came to fetch you when Arthur needed to speak with you.

"Hi Carla." Today was no different.

"I heard that Arthur was looking for me."

She nodded solemnly and beckoned to Carla to follow her, an order which Carla in turn dutifully obeyed. Arthur was a particularly intimidating individual. He was quite kind, in fact, for someone who oversaw a group of debt collectors. The two women padded their feet down the navy-blue carpeting which had been matted down from the hundreds of feet stampeding over it for years. Miriam took a left and sat down in her cubicle as Carla continued on forward and tapped lightly on an office door.

"Ahem, hmmm," she could hear Arthur clearing his throat from inside the office. "Come on in. Is that Carla?" He wheezed when he spoke.

"Yeah, Arthur." Carla pushed open the door. "It's me."

"Come in," he gestured for her to do so. "Have a seat," he wheezed.

Carla sat down in front of her aging boss. The only way she could think of Arthur was as being very long. He had a long face and a long bell shaped stomach that hung slightly over his belt. His dress slacks hung lazily on to his hips and bagged out, while a cream-colored, oversized button-down short-sleeved shirt adorned his upper body.

"You know why you're sitting here right now?"

""I think so."

"Look Carla, I like you. You're a nice girl."

"Thanks, Arthur."

Arthur leaned in forward, wheezing a bit more.

"Are you okay?"

"Oh, you know, it's this time of year. The allergies, my God! They're killing me."

"Well, summer's almost over."

"As if that's gonna be any better." His hands sprung from the desk in a desperate plea to the heavens. "Then we're gonna be in goldenrod season, I tell ya."

"I mean nothing can grow in the winter time."

"No, we can all just lock ourselves up inside with the dust. My daughter just *had* to get a puppy too."

"I don't suppose you're allergic to that as well?"

"Eight million kinds of dogs we could've gotten, and of course she picks a black lab. Next thing you know, I learn I'm sensitive to the dander that comes off of Labradors."

"Is there that specific of a thing with that?"

"Oh, you bet there is. I'll tell ya alright. It just never stops."

Carla was skeptical, but listening to Arthur list off his grievances meant that she would be putting off the impending negative review of her work. "It sure doesn't."

"Ehhh," he threw his hands up at her for a second time as though he was shooing her off. "You don't know, you've lived in Cambridge your whole life. Nothing grows in Cambridge."

"We have trees."

"Of course you do." He whipped a tissue out of it's box and gave it a hearty blow. "I suppose we should get around to what you're doing in my office right now."

"I suppose? Discussing the potential pollen count really did have its merits though."

"Carla, what's going on?"

She opened her mouth to protest, not entirely sure of what she was even going to say.

This didn't matter, as Arthur had an incredibly

clear plan of what he was going to say, "You were a killer! When you started that is. Boom! Skip after skip and you'd get them all. Now? Zilch."

Carla couldn't look Arthur in the eye. She knew he'd been waiting it out to yank her into his office and reprimand her. "It's just been a slow patch."

"You know you can't keep going on like this. You need to get back to the business of collecting on people's debt."

"I'm sorry, Arthur. I really am."

"I'm sure you are," he ripped off another tissue from the box and sneezed into it with such force she was sure he was about to cough up his own larynx, "but the fact remains- Achoo!" This particular sneeze sent a plume of spray up into the air between the two of them. Carla watched it dissipate, temporarily distracted. "Christ."

"It won't happen again."

"You can't let it. You're a nice girl. Maybe that's getting the better of you."

"I'm not nice." Carla looked at him determinately.

"Oh ho, yes you are. It's why it was so shocking when you actually managed to clock 'em in when you first started. You did. Left and right. I should've put money on you, but I was always a crappy gambler." Arthur wheezed out his words, wistfully looking to the window.

"Who put money on me?"

Arthur snapped back into attention. "Oh, I shouldn't've said that."

She shrugged. "Who cares now anyway?"

"Please, please go back to your desk and trace some skips?"

"I will." She looked him right in the eye.

"Please."

Incapable of promising Arthur for an umpteenth time, she left his office and made her way back to her cubicle, pausing slightly outside of Miriam's cube. "You put money on me when I started." Miriam merely twisted her mouth around and shrugged in response.

Carla's desk looked lonely, as all she'd left on it was her doodling in front of her desk top. Her will to do any more for the day was completely shot in the face after being called out by Arthur, even as lukewarm as he had been about it. She picked up the pad and stuffed it in her bag, which she slung over her shoulder. It was time to go home and at the very least get out of her monkey suit.

The bonus of leaving work early was that she beat all the commuters on the T, meaning she had a luxurious empty train car to herself and two MBTA workers swapping war stories about various acts of indiscretion they had managed to witness during their years working the red line. Boarding at Downtown Crossing, she had arrived home in record time, even for an off-hour. She skipped up her stairs, careful to avoid the busted step, and dropped her bag on her floor, looking around her little slice of the world. After stripping off the sweat soaked polyester and pulling on jeans that had been converted into cut-offs and a gauzy white string top, she pulled out her pad and stared at the words she had written. The tone was on a down turn, but that wasn't supposed to be how the song went. It was meant to be happy.

Carla lay on her back with her feet leaning on the wall forcing her body into an L-shape. She reread the words a bit more, thinking vaguely of scrapping them all. Her bed went into earthquake mode shortly thereafter, however, and she looked to one side and found her phone was signaling her to pay it some attention.

Hey what're you doing?

I knocked off work early today it was slow

Carla stared at the lie.

I feel like I haven't seen you in forever

I know me too She had attempted to balance all the

pieces of her life and thought she was getting away with it. Apparently not.

I wanna come by my mom's watching the store

That's cool I'm just hanging by myself

See you in a bit then

Carla plunked her phone down on her bed where it had been before and stared in its direction for a minute. Her mind returned to her lyrics and thinking about sailing ships took up residence once again in her mind. What had happened?

She wasn't able to ponder for too long. When Summer had said that she would see her in a bit, she must have really meant a very short bit. The rap on her door brought her back into reality. She sent her feet, which had remained leaning against the wall, to one side and let her body follow suit. She stood up off the bed with more agility than she'd normally give herself credit for.

The lock tumbled out of place as she twisted the knob about and it ended with a *thunk*. She wrenched the door open and waited as Summer strode in past her, holding a bottle of wine. "Glasses?"

"Well, come on in, Partner."

"Hey, don't give me crap. I brought you wine."

"S'pose I can't complain with that so much now, can I?"

"No mam, you can't." She put the wine down on Carla's one small square of counter. "Glasses?"

"I've got mugs." Carla shut and relocked the door, "So, what's up?"

Summer shrugged and opened the upper cabinet. "I just missed ya. Also, just wondering what's going on with you lately." She reached around for the mugs.

"How do you mean? It isn't like I totally fell off the map or anything." She'd been sure to try and balance everything.

"I don't mean like that." She came upon Carla's corkscrew, one of the few implements she owned that vaguely fell under that category of cooking. "I mean, I fell into a black hole when I met Jas at first. No hate here." She popped the cork off.

Carla lumbered to Summer's side and watched her pour a mug full of red. "Welp, then I can only assume you're using this as an excuse to drink with me."

Summer finished pouring her own mug and carried it to Carla's bed, where she sat down. Carla shifted her guitar from a chair to its proper home in a stand and sat down.

"We miss you."

"We've already established that I'm still around."

"But you aren't yourself. You're all mellow and low key and shit. It's weird."

Carla sipped her wine, "I think it's honestly just all the running around. I've been running to work, hanging with you, meeting up with Nico, I'm trying to write a song. It kinda all builds up."

"I get that." Carla could tell she didn't.

"I'm physically sleepy, you know?"

Summer nodded.

"It's really hard to sleep in someone else's bed."

"I swear Jas grows like nine extra limbs as soon as we get into bed."

"Yeah! That's it."

"How do they take up so much space? Even when they aren't that big, they just spread."

"Oh, my favorite is the diagonal sleeper. Like dude, you can have your side, but let me have mine. What? Do you think I turn into an amputee between the hours of midnight and six?"

Summer laughed and gulped. "I can't with that cause there's also the blanket thievery. Let me tell you, I love Jas, but two blankets on the bed at night is the secret to a happy marriage."

"If I ever make it there, I'll put that to the test."

"If you ever make it there?"

"Oh yeah, the forecast is looking cloudy."

"Explain." Summer squinted her eyes and sipped some more.

Carla wanted to beat around the bush, but she was too tired and too stressed. She didn't even have the wherewithal to get into her occupational woes at the moment. Hearing that aloud from her own lips would make those problems too real as well, so she kept it simple, "I wrote a not happy song lyric today."

The reception to this statement that registered on Summer's face told Carla that she had kept it a little too simple.

"I had been writing a song and it was all happy and I thought I was on a roll with something new."

"Are you sure this isn't the tired thing? It's just cropping up?"

"I dunno. I dunno if this whole thing is right, you know? He's really into things that I'd like to be really into, but I don't think I have the time and stuff." Carla was now getting frustrated with her own inability to articulate what she was feeling.

"Jas spent three hours the other day staring at some guy on YouTube so that he could learn to whittle and perfect his whittling techniques."

"Jas whittles?"

"No! That's the point. And, for that matter, neither do I, but it's all good cause we need to do stuff different from each other, you know?"

"Yeah, I get what you're saying."

"You don't seem convinced."

"He grinds his own coffee beans and then uses them to brew his own special coffee or something. It tasted like shit and I couldn't even tell him."

"Oh, is that like, a thing?"

"Yeah, he made a whole show about it."

"Well," Summer looked to be reaching for something to seem fair. "Maybe that's his one thing.

Everyone gets a thing. I have wrestling!"

"At least your thing means we got to stare at The Rock for a while."

"You make good points."

"Want more wine?" Carla was eyeing their mugs, as they had both polished them off.

"May as well kill the bottle."

Carla grabbed the mug and went to refill both of them. "Ah yes, no bottle left behind, an initiative I could always get behind."

"So he's a little bit pretentious with the coffee bean stuff. Whatever."

"Yeah, you know what?" Carla sipped a generous amount at once, "Whatever. Could be worse."

"Can't let little things bother you."

"I'm just not sure what we're doing. We're different in other ways I think, too."

"You can always just stop seeing him, you know."

"We have so much stuff we like though. Like music. That's a thing I always want in someone, music. We live near other, it's kinda convenient that way."

"A relationship of convenience is no relationship at all."

"Don't go throwing the R-word around." Carla returned one mug to Summer's hand.

"Oh, come on, it's been literally months and you've all but evaporated in that time."

"Okay, sure, but a relationship is something way else."

"Did you have the awkward talk even?"

"I don't believe in that."

Summer lifted her mug to her mouth, "Said the single girl."

"I don't like contrived things."

"You're dating a man who will only drink coffee he grinds himself. He's probably pen pals with the guy who sources the beans. Also, don't think I forgot about the fedora."

"I mentioned the fedora like one time."

"Yeah, that was enough. It's a fedora." Summer sipped, "Well, whatever, I wouldn't get your panties in a twist over some fedora-wearing guy you aren't even in a relationship with."

"You make many good points."

"I know, right? So then, since I've literally just thought of it, next order of business."

"Very official. Will there be meeting minutes later?"

"I'm not sure what that means, but the next order of business-"

"Is your business?"

"You mean the business my mother is desperately clinging to, which I'm trying to turn around and failing spectacularly at? Ehhh, wrong. Jas!"

"Why is Jas business?"

"Jas wants to enter a song contest."

"Sounds cool."

"Well, he isn't gonna do it alone. So you should do it with him!"

"He has a whole band."

"So what?"

"So he doesn't need me."

"When you do your writing, you're halfway decent."

"Why, you flatter me."

"So, just actually keep at it and make a song with him and the other guys. You'll have fun together."

"Seriously?"

"Yeah! And, like, let's be honest, you're the only one who can sing out of all of them."

"I prefer the guitar."

"Yeah, you are *highly* proficient at guitar. But also, they really need a singer. They don't totally know it, but they do… They'll learn that… Probably."

"I think you should stick to the bookstore-coffee shop business. Sales does not seem to run in your blood."

"Ahh see? Sometimes you make good points too!" Summer doubled forward giggling slightly.

"Maybe we should eat. Like food."

"I would love to eat, like, food."

"It's as though you're making fun of me or something. So unusual for you."

"Pizza."

Carla grabbed her phone and ordered via app, "So Summer…"

"So Carla."

"Speaking of the coffee-book-shop-store-thing, how's that going?"

Summer placed her now empty mug on the floor and sat up straight, "it isn't."

"No?"

"Well, I shouldn't say that. It just isn't right now. It's slow."

"Did you figure out how to make a business plan?"

"Yeah, I figured it out and all. I'm just not great with words. And all the sample plans had charts and graphs and data. I have none of that stuff, I don't even know where to get it. I know I need something though."

"Yeah, I think."

"You can't just sit and relax, because it'll all just go stale, you know?"

"The store?"

"All of it! Life! I need to build something. Otherwise I'll just wake up one morning and realize I'm schlepping in and out of work every day like a zombie, like, like-"

"Like me?"

"No, I don't mean-"

"I know what you're saying. I know, I get it."

Summer's shoulders relaxed. "Thank you."

"I don't have any of my wine here." Carla stood up and grabbed both now empty mugs, "We good to go run down the street?"

Summer looked in the direction of their potential path, but shook her head. "No, I wanna catch up with Jas again and actually spend some time with before we both fall asleep."

"I hear you." She walked to the sink and set the mugs down in there.

Summer stood up. "I'm sorry it was a short one."

"No sorries. Don't worry. I'll manage to get through the pizza somehow."

Summer walked to the door and opened it up. "See you later then?"

"Yeah, see you later."

Carla shut the door behind Summer and turned back to her sink. She ran the water and washed out the bottle, moving on to cleaning the mugs after. Searching for other mundane tasks, Carla came up short and she turned back around to stare at the pad of paper that still lay on her bed.

She lay back down on her bed and picked up the pad. She looked over the words she had written and hated every single one of them. They were all wrong, and her feelings had to be all wrong. She put pen to paper once more and watched what words would come out of it.

A foundation that I'd built so strong
The deck boards break shit I was wrong
I'm fearing choices that might get me wrecked

She hated that too. That wasn't how she wanted to describe anything, it was just what happened to come out. She was sparking all over the place, and the expectations she thought that one man might be able to fulfill weren't enough, as she had always believed they would be.

It was at this point that her phone went off yet again that night, and it was, of course, from Nico. Though the seeds of doubt had been sewn that morning, she couldn't resist his request to go to his place once again. Hoping that perhaps their last few conversations were a blip on the radar, she pulled on white sneakers to match her white top and picked up her bag. She considered filling it with clothes, but thought better than of lugging her crap all around town. If she brought an outfit now then she would have to lug what she wore currently all the way into work.

Carla looked down at her pad once more, knowing that nothing more of substance would come out of her tonight and certainly nothing of positivity. She picked up her phone and cancelled the pizza. Maybe after she went to Nico's tonight, this would be enough to send some different sparks all over the place. Uncertain of where she was going or why, Carla turned her back on her bed, her words, and her guitar. She set off for some now unknown territory for the night.

BYE BYE SYMPHONY

Sauce bubbled up in a cast iron pot. She wasn't much of a cook, but stirring things was always strangely relaxing. The noise of the bubbling sauce mixed with Carol King as she warbled about someone loving her tomorrow, but it was ultimately drowned out by the sound of several screaming middle aged women taking digs at each other on reality television. The medley created the perfect state of white noise that Carla needed to think about work, and Summer, and Nico. There was only one noise that could ever cut through and bring her into the present.

"Look at them."

Carla turned to watch a bleach blonde woman who was crisped to perfection show off her nine thousand dollar sunglasses to a camera, confessional style. The image almost immediately cut to that very pair of sunglasses being ripped from her hand and thrown into oblivion by a particularly aggressive brunette. "What? The sunglasses?"

"No," her mother gestured back at her wildly. "Look at that one, just throwing them across the room!"

"That's what I just said."

"You wouldn't believe these people. Always screaming and yelling at each other."

"You're watching real housewives. What else would they be doing?"

"Sometimes they do good things." Her mother became instantly defensive about women she'd never met, having formed the strongest of bonds through para-social relationships.

"Really?"

"Yeah! Really."

Carla gave her gravy one more stir, fearing it would stick, "Okay, lay it on me."

"They do a lot of charity work."

"Is it real charity work though?"

"What'd'ya mean? Why are you saying that?"

"Like, do you think they actually care about giving to charity, or do you think they just care about being seen giving to charity?"

"That's very mean spirited."

"How's that mean spirited?"

"You don't know that."

"I bet I do though."

"What's the difference anyway, though? Either way someone who needs help gets help." Her mother stared at her, waiting for a rebuttal. "Well…" she stared at Carla, "Hah!" She was victorious, "I stumped the brilliant Miss Carla."

"Whatever."

"Party for me."

Carla continued to absentmindedly stir and stare at the television. The scene had moved on to two other lanky blondes who were walking down a West Coast beach looking earnest and making apologies to one another. The sun was sinking down behind dunes and Carla forced her ears to pick out Carole King rather than their banter. Carole's cooing had a way of making a sunset look a lot more appetizing to listen to than, "No, I know, but" over and over.

"Oh, these two. Well, you wouldn't believe what they were doing in the last episode before they got into a fight."

Carla smiled bemusedly at her, "I don't know, Ma, what?"

"They were going into what looked like these stand-up showers. You know, like the nice ones you see where's no bathtub and just a glass cube?"

"Yeah."

"Except it was a circle and made of metal and there was steam coming out the top of it."

"Like a sauna?"

"No. It wasn't hot steam; it was steaming because it's freezing in there. These women, sheesh, can you believe it?"

"So they got into ice saunas is what you're saying?"

"Yeah, they call it cryo-something or other."

"Why?"

"Oh, who knows! You can never tell what's going on with those people out in California. They're all a little wacky, you know?"

"Yeah, I guess."

"Well, none of them just settle down, you know?"

Carla watched the sauce start to bubble up again and twisted the knob on the stove slightly to turn the gas down. "They're all married. They're literally called housewives. There have to be husbands otherwise they'd just be house…ladies?"

"Yeah, for now. It's always this one getting divorced and that one getting remarried for the fourth time."

"I couldn't see myself getting married for more than twice. It looks tiring," Carla kept the sauce moving so that it didn't have an opportunity to boil over, "and expensive."

"Well, it's not even about money, Carla." She spun to look at her, causing Carla to concentrate on stirring even more. Or at least as much as one could concentrate on moving her arm in a repetitive clockwise motion. "That's just no way to live. Look at your father and me-"

"Yeah." Carla could smell what was coming. It was wafting through the aroma of garlic and bay leaves.

"-or your sister and Nick-"

"Right." She was hoping if she slowly and loudly said affirmatives through her mother's words, that maybe she would get a hint. Or just stop.

"-you know? They're so happy."

Carla paused, wooden spoon in her hand and looked over at her mother.

"They had such a nice wedding."

"That was a circus." An unavoidable circus, but a circus nonetheless, and one Carla didn't envision for herself.

"A wedding is a party! It's a celebration!"

"A celebration that doesn't include the immediate world is also nice."

"Oh, there you go again being all negative."

Carla realized the sauce was bubbling with a vengeance, despite the heat being turned down.

"Your sister just looked like a princess. Don't you want to have your own day like that?"

Carla tried to start stirring again, "Big to-dos like that aren't my thing."

"I'd just like to see you happy with someone."

"Another Nick?"

"Nick treats your sister good, and he has a good job."

"There's not much more going on there though, is there?" Carla mumbled as the cast iron had grown too hot and a sauce bubble exploded at her. "Shit."

"Watch your mouth."

Carla moved the pan off the burner and killed the heat. "Sorry, Ma." But she wasn't sorry about either statement.

"Don't let that gravy sit off the heat too long."

"I know."

"You know how your father gets when it isn't just right."

"How could I forget?" The tracks were jumbled on the CD player and *It's Too Late* switched on now.

"Carla, just don't, please. I'm not in the mood right now."

She was fourteen and her mother was pouring the same red sauce recipe into small containers. "There, that's the problem." Carole King's voice, again, permeated the moment.

"The bottom?"

"It's burnt, but here." She scraped out the last bits of usable sauce into sauce containers and clunked the pot into the sink. "I can just package these. Use it for something else later. Lasagna or something."

Carla looked down at the thick layer of black, tar-like sauce that clung to the bottom of the pan. "Do you want me to wash it out?"

"Yes, Carla." Her mother was terse. "Wash it while I package these and throw them in the freezer. I need to run out to the shed and grab a new can of tomatoes."

"Okay, chill out."

"Don't start with me, young lady."

Carla turned on the hot water, grabbed a spatula, and got to work. She looked out the window as her mother scurried to their shed, getting flustered with every clotted footprint she left in the dirt behind her. She knew why her mom was so upset, and the fact that the woman was falling all over herself running around frustrated her to no end.

The texture of iron vibrating up through the metal of the spatula and into her hand notified Carla that she had scraped through to the bottom of the pan. She looked down at the chunks of burnt sauce swirling through the water. She wanted badly to just throw dish soap in the pan and be done with it. She knew that cleaning wasn't an option and as she looked back up at her mother returning to the house with cans of tomatoes under each arm, she found herself reaching for a can of salt for the same frustrating reason.

Carla turned off the water and coated the bottom of the cast iron in the salt, scrubbing furiously. It always grossed her out that the cast iron couldn't be cleaned with soap and had to be scrubbed and then seasoned. The one time she had attempted to use actual soap she was treated to a lengthy verbal berating and lectured about how the iron wasn't meant to be scrubbed with soap; it would ruin it, by her father. He had grown more and more irate with every word that he spoke to her as though she were an infant.

"Okay, I don't think he'll be home for another forty-five minutes. That'll give us enough time to whip up a new gravy. Might be a little acidic is all. But that's fine." She practically hip-checked Carla out of her way and grabbed the pot, rinsing the salt out over and over again.

"I'm sure it'll be okay."

"I just really don't need a lecture today, okay?"

"Yeah, yeah, fine." Carla held her arms up, defeated.

Carla watched her mom slam the pot back on the stove and squirt in olive oil. She crushed garlic on top of the sizzling oil, as nothing had really had the time to cool, and welcomed the aroma into her nostrils for the second time that afternoon. The cans were opened and her mother made sure to mix around the garlic bits before they stuck, ultimately introducing the crushed tomatoes into the pan. Moments later, basil leaves, oregano, and a bay leaf joined the party. The sauce, which had begun to bubble up, was now lowered to a simmer and Ana's shoulders slumped down to a relieved resting position. She turned to Carla, "Your new job is to stir. Don't let it burn. I don't have the patience to do this a third time today." The middle-aged woman leaned against the counter and rubbed sweat through her eyebrows.

"Okay, I'm on it."

Twenty minutes later and Ana jumped at a slammed door.

"Is that Dad? Is he home already?"

"I guess so. Here," her mom reached for a jar of peanut butter. "Just spoon a tiny bit in, it'll make it less acid-y. Last thing I wanna hear about is agita."

Carla sent a laugh in her mother's direction out of kindness, but it was obvious it accomplished little in the way of calming any nerves. She refocused on her new-found duty of stirring.

"You're home early!" Her mother said, flustered, as her father lumbered in. He clunked heavily down on one leg with every other stride.

"Is that a problem?" It seemed his brow had sunk lower with each passing year.

"No! Of course not," Ana's voice was over correcting. "We just wanted to make sure everything was ready.

Joe rubbed his hands together as though to clean them, though succeeded only in rubbing around the residual dirt of his workday. "I need to grab a shower anyway. Hey Carla," He gave her a quick peck on the cheek. He turned with slumped shoulders and made his way upstairs. Carla had learned the gait of his new walk perfectly by now and she tracked the beat of his footsteps into the bathroom.

"That didn't seem so bad."

Her mother merely looked up at her pointedly before returning to rushing about the kitchen. Twenty minutes later, Carla's mother placed a bowl of the gravy down on the table with a furrowed brow. It was nothing compared to what had been cooking for hours.

A freshly showered Joe, however, hadn't cared for the simple request to hold on for just a few moments longer, already annoyed at the fact he had to wait at all.

"So, Carla," He picked up a heaping spoonful of pasta and put it on his plate. "Where's your sister tonight?"

"I- uhh." Josie was most definitely at her boyfriend Robbie's, and though torturing her was a favorite pastime of Carla's, completely ratting her out wasn't on the to-do list.

"Oh, she went to her friend's and probably wound up at the mall or something," Ana said the words dismissively, perhaps hoping to fool herself as well as Joe. Carla knew her mom's radar was top notch. Specifics weren't known, but she somehow could just smell it whenever Carla or Josie had been up to something.

"Well, don't you think she should be here? It's family dinner."

"I think she just wanted to see her friends."

"Yeah? Well that's nice for her; maybe I'd like to see my friends too."

"I'm sorry spending time with us is so horrible."

"Hey! I work all day so we have enough. So that we can live in a house and this one can take guitar lessons. I'm tired. She can show up for family dinner and show some respect." He reached for the gravy and spooned heaps of it onto his pasta and chicken.

Ana's face slumped as she watched him cut up the food. "Sure Joe, I just thought-"

He sniggered under his breath, "Thought." Carla could practically feel the tension between her mother's scapulae as her shoulders cinched behind her back. They watched as Joe shoved a heaping fork of food into his mouth. He chomped at it sloppily and his lip curled but he said nothing. That was it, they could relax. Ana leaned back in her chair with slumped shoulders, relieved the episode was over.

"Oh shoot, I forgot the cheese." Ana popped up, with a little life returning to each motion. She stuck her head in the fridge and rummaged for a block of Pecorino Romano.

"Like it'd matter," Joe mumbled and glowered at Carla.

"That's weird," she stood up straight. "I must have more in the shed fridge." She walked out the backslider.

As soon as she left, Joe threw his fork on the plate. "Jesus, this is God awful."

"I think it's okay?" Carla knew not to be too overenthusiastic and also not to offer too much sympathy towards her mother. Had she, her father would've been on instant alert. The choosing of sides too blatant.

"Okay? Are you crazy? Why don't I just bring this down to work tomorrow? We can save on concrete 'cause I'm sure this'd do the trick."

"I dunno, I think it's alright." A useless defense.

"This tastes like shit."

"Bu-"

"Carla just shut up and don't defend her. I work all day and I have to come home to crappy food and a filthy Goddamn house."

"Why don't you just clean the house?" The words escaped as a mumble before she could shove them back inside her brain.

"It might have to come to that, Smartass." He practically spat at her.

Flinching was the only response she could muster at this point. Even a meager defense at this point would only prove to irritate him further. He could be even angrier with her mother, he could stop paying for her lessons. Her lessons were a life raft and she couldn't lose them.

"Nothing to say now?"

"N- no."

"Get out of here."

"What?"

"Go to your room, go to Summer's, I don't give a shit, I just don't feel like looking at you. Not when you're just ganging up on me with your mother."

"I'm not gangi-"

"GET OUT!"

Carla jumped from the table and ran to her room before her father could see tears in her eyes. She knew by this point her mother could see her leaving the kitchen and walking toward the front of the house. Her questioning rumble of a female voice through the floor boards confirmed this theory and the sparring voices that followed further confirmed this.

She picked up her guitar and practiced, she plucked the strings as quietly as she could. Too much, and they would buzz; not enough, and she wouldn't be able to block out the sounds of screams.

To this day, Carla wasn't sure the exact turning point in life that had led her parents to go from fun Saturday car rides to moments of stilted silence. As time continued to pass they bottomed out and became used to the idea that life had brought them together, they'd had two kids, and one of those had presented them with the gift of grandchildren. A constant source of joy and distraction from an otherwise vaguely tolerable existence with one another. What Carla did know was that it was always easiest to keep her head down, be agreeable and not make waves, and to always keep an eye on the gravy whenever she was home visiting.

"So speaking of your favorite child…"

"I love all my children equally and you'll never hear me say different." Her mother announced to the invisible court transcriber, who was present when it came to matters of official, emotional announcements.

"Right. Will she be gracing us with her presence any time soon?" Carla wanted to eat and then she wanted to return to her home. A quiet, nice home where there wasn't anyone keeping score of her and Josie's life milestones.

"Might just be the kiddos."

"What?"

"Yeah, she might have to work. Not really sure yet."

"Oh," Carla found herself a chair to sit in. "Well, they usually bring more to the table if we're being honest anyway."

"Carla!"

"I speak only the truth."

"You're bad."

"Maybe so." She fished her phone out of her pocketbook. *Hey you actually gonna come?*

I can promise that Joey and Antonietta will

How're you gonna get out of this one?

Same way I always do, say we both have to work

Seriously? She's on my ass today

Come on we need this

Carla didn't respond. If her niece and nephew were delivered, at least they could deflect attention.

I'm gonna drive them over now

Carla waited patiently and pretended to be consumed by something on her phone. Her mother, of course, grew irritated by this and continued to cluck more and more loudly about this one's Botox or that one's lip fillers all in an attempt to try and bring Carla back into a conversation.

Eventually though, Josie arrived and Ana went into Nonna mode, rendering her happy as a clam. Carla ignored her sister's well rehearsed excuses, the sound of which floated down the hall and into the kitchen. She waited for the little rug rats to run around the yard and for her father to lumber downstairs. They crossed themselves, they ate, Carla helped clean and it was time for her to say her goodbyes.

"Carla!" Joey came running after her.

"What's up buddy?" She crouched down.

"We want to come to your house!"

"Yeah!" screamed Antonietta. "We wanna come."

"Well, I don't live in a house you know."

"Yeah, you do!" Antonietta clunked her way forward to where Carla and Joey were positioned on the threshold. "Ma's picked you up there and you walked out of a house."

"Yeah, but the house I live in has a bunch of apartments in it. It isn't like here, it's little."

"We don't care," piped up Joey.

"Yeah, we wanna see your house."

"Ma said we could go to your house."

"Oh," Carla asked, "so *Ma* said you could see my house?"

"Yeah! She did!"

Carla blew out a sigh, exasperated. She looked at their young, bright eyes and the matching grins they had inherited from their father. "Fine," she rolled her eyes as she said it, but ultimately couldn't suppress a smile herself.

"What's fine?" her father asked.

"The kids are coming with me!" Carla's words were greeted by cheers from her niece and nephew and faces of dismay from both her parents.

"Is that safe?" her mother asked.

"Why wouldn't it be safe?"

"There's that broken step for one."

"Technically, it's only half a step."

"That's risky," her mother's mouth twisted.

"I've made it so far."

"And how would you get there?" her father piped in.

Carla looked at them, unable to tell if they were even serious, "…we would walk."

"Walk!" He pronounced it as though it were the most ludicrous word he had ever heard of in his life.

"Yeah, walk."

"You're gonna take two kids on a twenty minute walk?"

"We can walk!" Joey piped up.

"Yeah," Carla smirked, "they can walk. And you didn't care when Summer and I would go running off all day."

"That was different," her mother puffed up in her chest. And besides, that was a different time."

"Hardly."

"It's night!"

"It's seven and it's summertime. The sun is still out."

"We can walk!"

"We can! We really can and Ma said we could go."

"She did?" Her father raised a skeptical eyebrow.

The two little ones nodded repeatedly like synchronized bobble heads.

"Come on," Carla said. "Let's go explore my studio apartment!"

A chorus of cheers couldn't be fought with, not even by two grandparents, desperate to cling onto the little bursts of life that visited their home. The trio turned on their heels and Carla's parents were left to their own devices. Joey jumped ahead of the other two and started to hop from crack to crack, intent on making a game of even the most pedestrian of tasks.

Eventually, a few minutes into their walk, Antonietta asked, "What's your house like?"

"Yeah! What does it look like inside?" Joey shouted back.

"Well, like I said, it isn't all that big."

"Yeah, but you have a television, right?"

"And a kitchen and living room and a bedroom and stuff, right?"

"All the rooms are kinda like one big room."

"Why? Joey asked as he jumped from crack to crack.

"'Cause that's the best way they could fit together, my bedroom and kind of living room are at the front near a window and in the back is my kitchen and then my bathroom."

"That sounds squishy."

"It's only me. So it isn't too squishy."

"If me and Antonietta lived in a house that little with Ma and Pop we'd probably be kinda squishy."

"Lucky then that you don't, I guess."

Joey kept hopping from one foot to the other on every crack.

"That's rude."

"Thanks Antonietta, bang a left, Joey!"

Joey hurled his body in the wrong direction.

"Other left!"

"I got it!"

"See? I might have a tiny apartment, but at least I know my right from my left."

Joey made a muffled noise of defeat and Carla allowed him to lead them the rest of the way home, only giving him minor directional turns along the way. Her phone buzzed and she reflexively checked it should it be Nico. To her dismay, she saw it was her mother checking on her status.

Back before sunset. She sent the pointed message, regretting showing the woman how to text with each passing minute.

"Is that the broken step?"

"Yeap, hop on over it."

"Why don't you just fix it?" Joey jumped two

footed with all his might.

"That isn't mine to fix." Carla arrived next to him on the porch and fitted her key in the front door.

"But it's your house."

"Not really, it's someone else's house and I pay them to live here. So it's their step to fix." The trio began to climb the stairs.

"Why don't you just ask them to?"

"Because…" Carla trailed off; kids could be exhausting. She shoved a second key into the door to her unit. "Because then they'll raise the rent." She pushed the door open, waiting for another round of questions, but instead both children wandered into her little apartment, looking around with wonder. She supposed they'd never seen a place so small.

"Is this your fridge?!" Joey asked, his voice incredulous.

"That is a mini-fridge. Yeah."

"Why is it so small?"

"Well I can only eat so much in a week."

Antonietta looked around at everything else though and ran her hand down the wall as she walked toward the front of the studio. "This is your little home?"

"Yep, it's my little home."

"Do you have any ice cream?"

"Sorry Joey, shoulda stayed at Nonna's for that."

"Ma said we should come here though."

"Why?"

He shrugged his little shoulders, "I dunno. Can I watch T.V.?"

"If you want."

"Cool," he turned it on. "Hey!"

"What?"

"No Spongebob."

"Yeah, no cable."

Confusion spread across the boy's face. "How?" was all he could muster.

"I don't need it."

"But now what're we gonna do? It's too dark to go outside and you don't even have a yard!"

Antonietta broke into her brother's complaints by plucking the C string on Carla's guitar, sending a deep, friendly tone throughout the small space.

"That's usually what I do."

"This place is perfect." A smile spread across her face, completely contrarian to her brother's look of despair.

"Here," Carla reached in the back of her pocket and produced her phone.

Joey looked down on it. "Don't be fresh with me young lady!"

"What?" Carla exclaimed.

"That's what it says! From 'Ma.'"

"You can read?"

He looked up at her. "I'm seven."

"Oh," it was hard to correlate height and age and life milestones. "Well, play flappy bird or something."

"What's that?"

"Just entertain yourself." She was growing more intrigued by Antonietta's continual plucking of strings. She walked over to her. "You can pick it up and play it you know. Here," Carla grabbed the guitar off its stand, "sit on the bed."

Antonietta followed instructions and accepted the instrument as it was placed on her lap.

"Are you a righty or a lefty?"

"Righty."

"Cool, me too. So hold the neck," she helped position it appropriately, "in your left hand."

"Okay. Like this?" The guitar was enormous on Antonietta and she nearly disappeared behind it.

"Yeah! Just like that. Now, you wanna put pointer there," she arranged Antonietta's finger accordingly on the corresponding string. "That's your first finger, then your next finger goes here and then your third finger goes there."

"This kinda hurts."

"Yeah, but push down as hard as you can, okay?"

"Yeah."

"Okay, good, and now strum all the strings with your right hand."

Antonietta made one sweeping motion with her arm and sent a plume of warm noise out across the apartment. Joey was completely unmoved, but Antonietta smiled at what she had created. She tried again, but the sound wasn't quite right and the strings buzzed a bit. "Oh," she slumped.

"That's okay, you've just gotta hold those strings down as hard as you can. You made a G chord."

"I made it?"

"Yup."

She lifted her left hand away from the guitar for a minute. Imprints of lines had been carved into her flesh from the strings. Antonietta ran her thumb over them, feeling the little bumps. "Ouch."

"No worries. That's what callouses are for. Want to learn another?"

She bobbed her head up and down.

"Here," Carla went to work arranging her fingers into the cascading pattern of a C chord.

"This is what you went to school for?"

"Wha-?" She had been wrapped up in their impromptu lesson; the question caught her off guard.

"Ma said you went to college."

"She told you that?"

"Yeah, and she told us you could make music."

The idea that Josie ever told her kids anything about Carla at all hadn't much occurred to her. Josie was always so wrapped up with running around here and there and popping in at dinner only to push her buttons. "Yeah, I went to a school for music. But only for a little bit."

"She said that too."

And there it was. "Well, it just. It didn't make sense at the time? You know?"

"Umm." Antonietta giggled sheepishly at her aunt and them strummed the guitar sending out a lower bellow this time. "No?"

"I loved music. At some point though, I had to decide what I was really doing and-" she had to halt what she was saying. Antonietta was looking at her out of enormous brown eyes, clear and blank, because she hadn't yet arrived at an age of discrimination and preconception. "I just wanted to do something that would set me up for a nice life."

"Do you like your job? What you do now instead? Ma tried to explain it but I didn't really understand."

"It isn't music, but it's fine."

"Then why is it better?"

"Because, I'm comfortable."

"But you just said it isn't better than music. *And* you said you love music."

"It's complicated?" she tried.

Antonietta screwed up her face as she pressed the strings into the neck one more time and strummed.

"Nice. What about you though, what do you wanna be when you grow up?"

"I dunno, I could cut hair like my mom."

"But do you like playing with hair?"

"I don't really care."

"Well, then maybe we should find you a different job?"

"Maybe you should find a different music job?"

"Touché."

"I don't really know what that means." Antonietta gave up on chords and went back to picking at random strings as her fingers had started to turn purple from pain.

Carla sat back and watched her experiment further, wondering if Antonietta would take to the guitar as she had around the same age after being shown some tricks by her uncle. Joey had been zoned out for quite some time at this point and immersed in his own world of iPhone games. It wasn't long after that a knock on the door signaled the arrival of her sister.

"Well, nice of you to join us," Carla shot at her sister upon opening her door.

"Hey, we needed it," Josie whisper growled back at her. "Did you guys have fun with Carla?"

"I played games!"

"Nice," Josie raised an eyebrow at Carla.

"I played the guitar!" Antonietta proudly announced, and Josie's eyebrow fell back down.

"You did?"

"Yeah, she showed me some chords."

"You wanna come back and play some more another time?" Carla asked.

"Yeah!"

"Well, you let me know and we'll do it. Whenever you want."

"I think it's time to go, guys. Carla looks tired."

Antonietta slid the guitar off her lap and onto the bed, while Joey flung her phone to one side and scampered out the door with a screeching, "Bye!" He waited in the hallway. Antonietta followed suit, first offering her aunt a hug.

"Get in the car while I say goodbye."

"Okay!" Joey said, "Oh, Carla, you kept getting messages."

"What?"

"You could have peeled yourself away from the games and told her, Joey."

"They were from someone called Nick-o." And with this pronouncement, he and Antonietta went clomping down the stairs.

"Watch out for that step!" their mother yelled down to them. She twisted her head back around to look at Carla, smirking. "So who's Nick-o?"

"Nico."

"Why is Nico texting you on a Sunday night?"

"Does no one ever text you Sunday night?"

"Who is he?"

Carla sighed, "He's just someone I'm… seeing." Labels confused her.

"So he's your boyfriend?"

"No!" She supposed that sort of gut reaction could assure her that that label wasn't on the table.

"So he's your hookup?" Josie's voice spewed disappointment at that statement.

"Don't you have children waiting in the car for you?"

"Well, I know you aren't just friends. You don't have those besides, like, two people."

"I have friends who aren't Summer and Jas!" Her sister was right though, Nico wasn't a friend. They spent too much time together not just hooking up and she listened to him expound on way too many personal details of his life to just be friends.

"Nope. No you don't."

"So where were you?"

"Getting some time to myself." She said it pointedly. "And don't try and change the subject."

"I'm not changing anything. Just wondering how I became an impromptu babysitter for the night."

"Is spending time with your niece and nephew so horrible?'

"Is spending time with your whole family horrible? Nick hasn't even been around for dinners in forever," Carla matched the newfound intensity in Josie's voice.

"I thought it'd be nice if my kids could hang out with their aunt instead of Mom and Dad for once, for obvious reasons. And, if we're keeping score, why don't you bring around this *Nico* guy. God forbid we ever meet anyone you date."

"Unlike some people, I don't jump into things too quickly."

"You don't have to jump too quickly into anything, just grow up or settle down or something. Jesus, look at you. How are you even happy?" She motioned to Carla's studio before turning on her heel and exiting.

"Hey, I am happy. Don't put your shit onto me," Carla yelled at her. "And by the way," she raised her voice, the farther downstairs Josie went, "they call it settling *down* for a reason." She slammed the door, irritated with the turn the night had taken. Getting ditched for a family dinner, unexpected childcare, probing into her life, and of course, being told that she wasn't happy. Because of course, in Josie's world, the only way Carla could be happy was if she was trying to chase after the same things as Josie.

She'd forgotten about Nico's texts for a beat as she fumed over the past five minutes, which had escalated rapidly. She looked down at the messages. He was having a rough night. He wanted to see her. She needed a distraction and was happy to push any misgivings she was having aside. She let him know she would be there in moments. And let her front door slam behind her as she set off for his place.

The walk had left her hot inside with cool, wind-burnt skin. Nico's apartment felt uncomfortably warm.

"Wow, are you all good?"

She walked into his apartment with steam practically radiating off of her. "Yeah. Yeah, I'm fine." She sat down on his couch and looked around the apartment. The counter was laden with used dishes that had piled up, and another sat on the table in front of her next to a small bong. The clutter caught her eye and she found it distracting. Even annoying. "Actually, no." Maybe everything was annoying her right now. "My sister ditched me with her kids and then we had this sort of argument."

"That sucks," he sat down next to her.

"You know when someone just pushes their shit on you?"

"Totally."

"Like, don't tell me I'm not happy with how my life i-"

"That's the exact problem I'm having right now."

"Huh?"

"Yeah, with my bandmates. It's been killing me. It's why I needed to see you tonight. I needed someone to understand."

He'd caught her off guard. "Your bandmates?" She tried to squelch the deadpan element in her voice.

"Yeah, they can't understand where I'm coming from with what I need. They're squashing my voice. My sound."

"And you've spoken to them about it?" She didn't need to talk about band drama, she'd wanted to complain about her sister. But this new diversion was taking over.

"Yeah, you know who the problem is in all this, it's Jamie." Nico leaned forward with his elbows balanced on his knees.

"Why Jamie?"

"Well," Nico looked at Carla, aghast, "I told you before. He didn't even like my inclusion of bongos into our Beatles covers that night."

"Oh yeah. The night we met." She didn't have the heart to tell him that absolutely no one on earth needed the bongos included in the song, *Come Together*, but this didn't seem to be the moment.

"What? Oh yeah, right."

"So did you guys have an outright fight?"

"The problem with Jamie is that he doesn't understand *true* creativity. It's what makes the earth move.

He just hasn't suffered, you know? Like truly been in pain ever. That's what the problem is."

"So you think to make art you have to suffer and Jamie hasn't suffered?"

"Exactly."

"But you've suffered? So is that what you argued about?"

"Jamie is terrible at communicating. He's negative. He just says no all the time. Constantly, it's exhausting."

"I don't know about Jamie. But, I've heard you play and I've heard you sing." Carla nearly rolled her eyes as the words flew from her mouth. "And you're great, you don't need to rely on others. But, I'll say it's just nice to have people to work with and bounce your ideas off of. You know?"

"No. I don't know. I don't think you understand. Jamie is stifling me."

"I do. I do understand. Other people shooting you down sucks, it's frustrating."

Nico leaned back. "It's fine Carla," He let a hand fall on her leg. "You don't have to try and get it."

"But I do get it."

"I think you share one thing with Jamie. You don't give into sadness. You know?"

"No. I don't think I know."

"Well, you haven't really felt pain or loss. Not the way I have."

Carla was so taken aback; words escaped her. "Sorry?"

"Well, it isn't the way I've felt loss. Like when my grandparents died or when I lost my dog as a child. I saw his body; it needed to be scraped from the street after that car hit him. I can't live closer to where all the other students live right now because my parents would only pay for *this* apartment. It's just another thing to alienate me from everyone else."

"That's the loss Jamie and I haven't felt?"

"Or you. You've never told me anything about pain you've felt. You should really explore that more."

"I have loss." In fact, she'd been planning on telling him about her frustration this very night.

"I think if you really took that time to dig into that, you could maybe even get to a place where you could return to school."

"I had to leave school because of-"

"It was a smart choice for you. You at least knew that you don't have enough life under your belt."

"But that wasn't the reason."

"You're very smart to have done that.'"

Carla sat back and stared at the television. She wanted very badly to say something, to recalibrate and gain her druthers. But her feelings hadn't made it into the rest of her brain. They were bound up in her chest, so she couldn't even be sure of what they were.

She sat still in his apartment. She still thought about what Josie had said. She thought about her happiness and about what she was doing with her life. She'd been in a holding pattern for the last few years. Devoid of real music; full of meaningless hookups. There was consistency, but it had always felt like a pit stop. No upwardly mobile career, no man she wanted to marry, and she never even dared to think about owning property. No one could even do that these days. Maybe a person like Nico could, but even then, it wouldn't have been his money, now would it have?

They still had some bad sex that night, which she tolerated until Nico was done and he rolled over to his side of the bed. Carla laying awake, pondering her ability to make a change, to tolerate a person's flaws in order to stay with them long-term, to tolerate apathy towards a career so it could pay off for her long-term. She dreamed of complacence with the notion of settling *down.*

RELAX, TAKE IT EASY

It was this overwhelming notion that one had to be miserable to produce a piece of truly beloved art that had constantly been glorified throughout the student body on her campus. She looked around at one girl in particular who had pronounced most dramatically that she'd had a long battle with anxiety and depression. That it was this that had led her to pour herself into her craft.

It wasn't that Carla hadn't ever lost anything in life or been denied what she desired, but she had applied to school to pursue music with a degree of naiveté, which had been promptly broken into pieces upon her actual attendance in classes. She had greedily ripped open her letter which had arrived in a full packet form that let her know she had gained admittance and the date that her first installment of money was due. The cash mattered not to her. She had always tolerated the basic parts of school so she could get to her ultimate goal, only enjoying the bits she wanted. That had arrived. Now all she would ever need to do was play her guitar and learn about music.

As the months wore on and she juggled working

her restaurant shifts on top of courses, her once resolute level of confidence had begun to bend and fold. These other students plodded in and out of class, looking as though they had just rolled out of bed or planned to roll back into one shortly thereafter.

So when she stared at this girl who had, as Carla so believed, the luxury of acquiring the attribute of anxiety, which could then be poured into her art, she became awash with jealousy. Carla didn't have anxiety, she had an accumulating pile of bills to pay. She was too busy trying to curb her debt to focus on whatever else on this earth could possibly be plaguing her. She looked at this girl, who had heaped perfect ringlets into a messy bun on the top of her head and sat there with a forlorn expression on her face. She wrote her notes in a Moleskine and tapped her brown, combat booted foot against the leg of her desk. At the end of the day though, her boots were Guess brand, her hair color wasn't from an at home bottled job, but one that probably cost hundreds of dollars and copious amounts of foil, and Carla had overheard her several times, talking about her uncle in LA, who worked as a producer for a record company. This was a person who could surely churn out piece after piece. She could spend endless hours perfecting her work. She had the gift of time being on her side and of an easily trodden path that lay before her.

As the day's lesson had ended, Carla stood up, elated to have no shift to work that night. She plugged ear buds in and set the song on her phone to "La Breeze" by Simian. The tempo of the song pounded a steady rhythm into her ears as she walked outside. She found herself accidentally charging her way to the subway as her feet couldn't help but hit every single beat. The final release came as the lead singer unleashed a wailing cry through the percussion heavy song.

She boarded the train but couldn't stop thinking of the girl in her class. Carla looked back down at her guitar, which she had taken to carrying with her in general, just in case she ever found herself wanting to sit and enjoy the day, and maybe play some tunes in the Common or on the Esplanade. It never seemed to happen though. She was too tired, or her head was busy thinking about something else, or her presence was needed by her family, mainly Josie, or her job.

She hit replay on the song yet again; the vibes were just right. It was a song to be played for sweeping decisions. By this time, she had hit Park and needed to change onto the red line.

She took stock once again of what had become her daily routine, of all the shiny dust that wore off her now that she was living in a day-to-day routine. What was she even learning here? Why couldn't she just do it herself? The subway car emerged into daylight as it stopped at MGH. It took off once more and rolled slowly over the Longfellow Bridge. The fact of the matter was that it had taken her eight months to realize that there was no uncle in Los Angeles waiting with so much as a janitorial position for her, let alone a substantial career opportunity. She would always be tired, worn down, and stressed out by going to school and waiting tables full time. Most of all, she would have the weight of six figures worth of debt by the time she concluded her studies.

Carla hadn't realized it in that moment as she watched the Prudential Center, Hatch Shell and Citgo sign whizz past her, how routine this view would become to her. The conclusion she had arrived at was that studying music full time for four years was a dream for some people to live out, but not one for her. Acceptance into the program had seemed infeasible, but it was ultimately attendance that would be her greatest hurdle overall. Carla looked once more at her guitar and vowed to herself that she wouldn't stop studying her music, writing her songs or give up what she loved. For now though, it was time to let a dream die. It would ultimately be the crux of her issue, which careened her into a new career path. Debt.

As her train car reentered a tunnel, "La Breeze" faded out one more time.

Carla hadn't attempted any contact with Nico, or anyone, for that matter. The last week had been one that consisted entirely of going to work and returning home. Every day she sat there in her cubicle, oblivious to most everything. She half-heartedly placed her calls. None of them panned out though. Cat man distracted her with talk about how Guccibear was doing in his recovery before pronouncing her to be a huge bitch and then abruptly hanging up on her. Greta would tell her about the virtues of squalene oil before following suit. Tim would come by and make a joke or two with her. She would dodge Arthur and his wheezing, as she couldn't take another minute of him imploring her to do her job and successfully nab a skip.

She found it was comfortable at home; she could curl herself on her bed and doodle or write. She took a page from Josie's book and skipped Sunday dinner. Texts were ignored and friends blown off. Nico hadn't even reached out. Carla had grown accustomed to him doing all the work, but that wasn't happening anymore either. Not being particularly thrilled with their prior discussion, she'd accepted the absence of communication freely as "La Breeze" reappeared on her journeys home over the Longfellow. That warm summer day that had existed so long ago floated back to her repeatedly on waves of sound. Ones that once filled her with energy, but now existed only as melancholic vibrations.

The actual vibration of her phone came to her once again after she found herself face-planting in full work gear on her bed. This silence she'd found herself in, particularly throughout the weekend, was her only incentive to pay attention. What surprised her was that it wasn't Josie bitching her out, nor was is Summer trying to get ahold of her for the umpteenth time, but Jas. It was sheer confusion that compelled Carla to answer.

As she came to learn, he asked to meet her at the Purple Salmon, to which she replied that she would because at the very least there would be a beer in it for her. It was upon her arrival that she found only Jas sitting at the bar by himself.

"Howdy," her voice nearly cracked, as it hadn't been in use for quite a bit.

"Hey partner." He opened his arms wide and she allowed herself to be enveloped in a bear hug.

"Can I get a Sam Adams?" Carla asked the bartender and perched herself on a stool.

"Thanks for coming to hang."

"I was surprised to hear from you. I mean, it's just…"

"Yeah, Summer usually makes the plans. You've been kinda off the radar. Again."

"Is that why I've been summoned here?" Carla accepted the beer that was placed before her.

"Only kinda."

Carla laughed and sipped. "But still kinda?"

"You can't keep blowing people off. You and Summer are more sisters than you and Josie are half the time."

She looked at him while he looked straight forward. It was an awkward topic for him clearly. "I know, she talked to me about this already. I know I keep doing this."

"Well, stop doing it then." He looked at her. "Is everything okay with you? 'Cause we've been friends for a while and you don't do this. Not like this."

"Well, honestly Jas," no, nothing was quite right at the moment. There wasn't a way of saying that. "It's just a kind of quarter-life crisis situation."

"Unless you plan to live until you're, like, a

hundred or whatever, I say you're too late for that excuse. Your man gotcha down?"

"Yeah, a little bit. Something he said the other day. It just bugged me 'cause it got me thinking about how I left school. I don't even know what I'm doing now. I mean, I know what I'm literally doing and why I had to leave. But collecting other people's debt really doesn't do it for me, you know?

"You never went to school to learn to be a debt collector, you went for music. That's what you need to do."

"That's what I keep thinking about."

"Why the disappearing act then? You don't need to, you've got us. We've got a song contest to enter."

"Sometimes, you know, you just have to decompress." She slugged down more beer.

"And what is Nico saying that has you think about that stuff?"

"Something was wrong inside his band. Then we got to talking and I got to thinking."

"What did he say when you told him what was happening on your side?"

Carla didn't want to admit that her side had been shut down moments after her entrance into his apartment. "He talked about how he's felt similar sometimes."

"So he talked about himself?"

"Yeah, I guess," Carla didn't want to repeat what he actually said.

"Well, I guess it didn't help."

"Why's that?"

"You said you've been avoiding everyone."

"Yeah. Plus, usually I hear from him. I haven't heard anything now."

"He always hits you up?"

"Yeah, it's familiar."

Jas looked at her for a beat. "Oh Jesus, are you talking about Paul again?"

"Well, come on. That was his move."

"No, his move was showing up when it was convenient for him."

"Maybe. But the thing he'd always say when he showed up was that he thought I was the one who wasn't interested."

"That's an excuse."

"But maybe I'm just doing that again. I mean I never make the plans. I just wait for the plans to happen."

"But Carla, look at Paul. Paul is like Nick, Nick is who Josie married. And that's not you. And that's not me or Summer."

"But maybe this time. Like this one time I should just try. I never try for things any more. I just wait for them to happen to me."

"Try for this. Write a song. Even just the lyrics. Bring it to me and we can do it together. We can go into the contest. It'll be fun and it'll give us both some legs."

"You're right."

"And call Summer."

"Yeah." Her neck grew hot with guilt. "I'll call."

Jas stood up and threw some cash on the bar. "I've got this one. Now," he opened his arms once again for one more hug. "I don't get what's up with Nico, but you have the worst taste in men, so it sounds like maybe that should go on ice." He let her go.

"And I'll send you some words."

"And Summer."

"Yeah, and Summer."

"We love you," he strode toward the door, "but, like, don't be a dick." He smiled as he left the building.

Carla estimated there were roughly two long slugs left to her beer. Two slugs worth of time before she chose her next move. Two slugs and call Summer? Two slugs and try to write? Two slugs and go home?

She took one slug. A little closer to the end of her beer and no closer to a decision. It was later, so surely at this point calling Summer would be a fruitless venture. She was too tired from work that day and couldn't bring herself to produce anything more. One more slug and the beer disappeared. The decision, as it had been all week, was to go home.

Naturally, as Summer and writing and work had been the only three things on her mind, it was at that particular moment that the man who she hadn't heard a peep out of for over a week, reared his head. Each LCD infused word bore holes into her pupils. So of course he wanted her to go over. Everything that had been convenient for Paul was being made as easily convenient for Nico. She was doing it again. It wasn't late, but she was tired. On the other hand, curling up in solitude for the week had been nice, but it would also feel nice to not feel lonely. Despite how lonely being with him had started to feel.

Their last meeting had ended that morning and she'd left without a second glance. But as she looked at his text, it had an almost pleading tone, if texts could even have those, she thought that maybe, just maybe, this meeting could go a little more smoothly. Maybe they wouldn't be a perfect fit, but maybe he could do her the favor of being kind. People have off days. Sometimes they have off weeks. With a decision consciously made, Carla set off in the direction opposite of her home. Her polyester pants made a swishing sound with every step.

When Carla arrived at Nico's place, she knocked her hand into his door several times. There wasn't anyone to answer. She stared at the door, her brows furrowed, until it occurred to her that anyone else witnessing this scene would think her to be insane. She knocked her balled fist against his door once again with more gusto, fueled largely by irritation. *What the hell?* She thought. She took out her phone.

I'm here.

She'd hit the send button quickly and then volleyed in her head about whether or not the punctuation was overkill. Another minute passed and Carla sat down on the top stair. She reopened his texts to her. *Come over. I need someone to talk to. I haven't seen you in a while.* They'd gone back and forth but each response he sent her indicated he wanted her there. So it couldn't have been her imagination. He'd wanted to see her. Her sanity check was complete. But, again, it made no sense. He'd made the effort to reach out, but now, nothing.

She stood, but was able to take only one step down. A door to the outside world had slammed and there she waited as he strode up and towards her. The edge of his lips curled upwards into a smile when he saw her, or maybe it was a smirk? "Were you waiting long?" His eyebrows cinched together.

"No. Not really."

"Oh. Well, come on. Come in." He rustled past her, jiggling around with his keys and opened the door. She followed him in. The whole space had been completely organized from the last time she'd been there.

"Wow."

"Wow what?"

"The place looks good. It looks like you straightened everything out."

"Ah yeah, well I had people over so."

"Right." She dropped her bag on the floor by the door. "So what's wrong?"

"What do you mean?"

"You said you nee-"

"Oh that was totally over with like the second after I texted you."

"Okay. So you just wanna hang?" she asked, but he'd been flying around behind the kitchen island grabbing glasses and liquids like a mad scientist.

"It was just this dumb disagreement with Jamie again. He saw that I was right though. I'm just over only having English in our songs."

"What do you want in there?"

"Carla," he looked up at her with a facial expression bordering on astonishment. "You know I can speak the two most beautiful languages on earth. Russian and German. It'd be a shame to not include bits of them." He held of the shaker he'd been concocting his beverage in.

Carla tried to reach into the recesses of her memory for mention of either language and was coming up empty on that front. "Right," was all she could manage.

Nico poured two glasses and brought them over to her.

"Oh no, sorry," she said. "I'm really good, I actually already had a beer, I kind of just want to chill."

"No! But I infused this tequila with jalapeno myself. Please just have one drink with me."

"I gotta work tomorrow."

He'd set one glass down on the coffee table and sipped the other, "Right, the pants."

"My pants?"

"Yeah, you always wear those *pants*."

"Is that a problem?"

"They just look so… I dunno, stiff?"

"Well, these are work clothes. It's about as comfortable as it gets." She tugged a little self-consciously at them.

"Oh, maybe just be a little less comfortable then?"

"Yeah," she grabbed the drink, changing her mind. "Probably won't." One more slug for the night. This one stung her lips and tongue, and fire slid down her throat. After she came up for air, her upper lip curled involuntarily. It was one of the most revolting beverages she'd come across in a while. Years of training from her parents to not talk with your mouth full and be polite kicked in and she instinctually said nothing.

As she tried to gulp back down her own saliva to keep from getting sick, Nico had clearly taken these gulping sounds as a sign of appreciation. "I know," he said, looking straight ahead, "it's delicious right? God, I love this stuff." Carla watched in horror and he dumped more into his mouth. He clicked the television on and the two sat back. Carla was left to ignore the flashing images and mute the sounds with her mind as she pondered what it was she was doing there and reflected further on Jas' earlier words. By the time she'd resurfaced, it was late. Nico had draped an arm over her shoulders and let his head roll in her direction, the signal to her that he was in the mood. The last time they had been together had left her dissatisfied and she'd hoped that tonight things may have improved. Maybe that way something in life could start running smoothly. They were fully into the cover of night, she had no fresh clothes with her for tomorrow, she was tired. But, home felt so far away now and Carla knew she wasn't going anywhere that night but one room over. Maybe just one more night could divert them away from the direction they were careening toward.

Carla had been awake since it was pitch black in Nico's room. She lay there with her back to him, staring out the window, waiting patiently for light to start peeking through the blinds. Summer. Work. Music. Jas. She rolled onto her back and looked over. Nico. She wanted to leave now and run back to her apartment, but it was still dark and that would've been rude.

She bounced around in the bed, foolishly hoping that maybe it would wake him up and that maybe he'd either entertain her or at least it'd give her an out to leave. Clearing her throat loudly turned out similarly negative results. She gave up and reached for her phone. It hurt her eyes to even look at the screen, but her mind wouldn't allow sleep to come to her. She scrolled through Instagram. Photos of puppies intertwined with musical artists at their concerts were all that occupied the feed. Occasionally, Summer and her books would sneak in there though. A picture of the store, a picture of her, a picture of a steaming coffee mug on books. That last one was the pause she needed. Carla wouldn't even know what to tell someone had they asked her the status of Summer and her plans. Had she even sorted out a business plan yet she wondered, unsure.

It was at that moment Carla pushed herself up to a sitting position and looked over at Nico. She could leave him a text and walk out the door; she needed to go home and change. She needed to go to work and collect the debt of others with the ferocity she once had when she herself was deep into the red. She needed to talk to Summer. Nico could be there later and he probably wouldn't even notice if she left now.

She pulled on her uncomfortable swishy polyester pants and wrangled herself back into the button down top she had arrived in.

Hey I needed to get into the office early. Let's hang out tomorrow or something?

She sent the text and saw it light up his phone; it had been buzzing all night and the evidence of other messages flashed across the screen. This one, like the others, did nothing to wake him up. She bent over, picked up her purse where she'd lazily dumped it the night previous. Or was it earlier that night? Everything had blended together and rendered her in a half-waking state. It was at this point that she felt a hand reach out and grab her leg. She nearly slapped Nico he had startled her so much.

"Jesus," she clutched a hand to her chest.

"You're going?"

"Yeah, I gotta run home before I head into work."

"Oh, that sucks."

"Yeah." *Some of us have to actually work for a living,* she thought. "Sucks."

"I wanna see you later though."

"Definitely."

He pulled her down to the bed and pressed his lips into hers for a long soft kiss.

"I'll see you." She stood up once more, purse in hand, and found her way to the door. She looked back on the apartment as the outside world had finally begun to light it up a bit and the grey of the outside bounced off all the walls and gleamed on reflective surfaces. She looked through the wall to where he slept before walking out the door and yanking it shut behind her.

Carla's eyes squinted at the light as she took her sunglasses off upon entering her office. The iced coffee she had grabbed on her way to work had done nothing to wake her up and, if anything, had achieved the direct opposite.

She stood in the back corner of the grey, fluorescently lit elevator and bided her time until the doors would slide open and she would have to hurriedly dart to her desk. Another run in with Arthur felt imminent and she wasn't in any mood for it. She had to turn everything around at work as part of her damage control plan for her life. She would relax, get her work done. and ignore the last couple weeks. She had a job to do and a day to grab by the balls. No person and no task could ruffle her feathers. The doors chimed out at her as they slid apart and she flew so quickly to her cubicle it could've been a teleportation.

Sitting low in her chair within the safety of her felt walls, she started up her computer and eyed the phone. She knew who she'd have to follow up with to make an impression. Hannah Daugherty.

With slumped shoulders, Carla opened up the appropriate files on her computer and eyed the phone one more time. Hannah was waiting on the other end of the line, surely. Possibly depending on Carla to call her. The thought did, however, cross Carla's mind that the best work wasn't done immediately upon her arrival at the office. That maybe to get her mind properly up and running she should take fifteen minutes to explore something else. That way, she'd be more prepared, surely. So this morning it would be business plans she'd look at. Summer needed one and Carla hadn't caught up with her properly in so long that she didn't even know how far in this endeavor Summer had made it. But, out of sheer curiosity, Carla went on a cyber-journey into the world of business plans.

It was around the time Carla had become fully immersed in the part concerning historical success and future projections that she realized she was nearly into the afternoon and had yet to pick up the phone. She grabbed at it quickly as though someone had been actually staring at her and she needed to convince them she'd absolutely been a contributing productive employee. She dialed Hannah's number and sighed deeply.

"Hello?" A voice suspiciously answered on the first ring.

"Hello, Ms. Daugherty?"

"Yes? Who's calling?"

"I'm looking to speak with you about a very large sum of money you owe to Macy's."

"Oh Carla!" A warm richness in Hannah's voice cut through her initial alienated tone. "You should have just said it was you."

Carla would've wavered. Not this time; she was determined to close this… Again. "Look, we really need to get into a payment plan Ms. Daugherty. It's only going to continue to get worse."

"Listen to you, Dear. Ms. Daugherty. I thought we

broke through that a while ago. Just call me Hannah."

"Right, Hannah. About the b-"

"Do you know what I just saw on the television this morning? A man making the most extraordinary cakes."

"Sure."

"I just can't remember what he was called. I think it was Cake Man? No that isn't right. Cake Maestro? Maybe. No, that doesn't feel right either."

Carla sighed, "Cake Boss! You're thinking of Cake Boss. But abo-"

"Oh! That's right! The Cake Boss. Well you know what really gets me about that show, other than that Leaning Tower of Pisa cake? It's the family. Oh they are just wonderful in it, you know?"

Carla could have mouthed the final words and she knew where Hannah was going with his next.

"Of course it's about more than just cake. What could be more important than family? Well, I guess I know someone who could think of something. Roger and his God-awful obsession with clamming. I just do not understand it?"

"Yes Ms. Da- Hannah."

"Just throws all our money into clamming, like that's going to be profitable in anyway. Then of course there was the red-"

"Tide. Mmhmm yes, I know. That's terrible luck. But if we could just return to the problem at hand."

"The problem at hand is that my monster of a husband sunk our entire fortune into a clamming business at the height of red tide. And then, to boot, he left me! Without a trace. Couldn't've been bothered to tell me. Have you ever had that happen, Carla? Do you know the pain that is?"

Carla felt her shoulders slump downward, almost as though in a choreographed manner. "Yeah, I've been ghosted before. Twice actually."

"Twice? Oh my God. It's an epidemic."

"By the same guy if you can believe it."

"See that's what I like about you Carla, you understand."

"It's painful."

"I know. So now I'm left here by myself. I moved my life to the East coast for Roger and then Roger just had to move away from me, probably with his fucking clams. Pardon my French. Now look at me, I have nothing and no one."

"To be fair, you do have a closet full of premium labels you bought at Macy's."

"And I have you!"

"Sorry?"

"Well, I do find it so sweet that you call so often to check in on me. It's nice of you to let me rant on how I do."

Carla's mouth fell open. "That's no-" she cut herself off. She was only calling for debt collection purposes, but it seemed almost cruel to tell a woman, who was clearly very lonely, this fact.

"Anyway, I really don't have the money to pay those people and I shouldn't have to, Roger should. It's his fault that I'm even in this predicament to begin with."

"Well, that may be the case bu-"

"Oh listen to me going on and on about this. So negative of me to do. Let's move to a different topic. I really should tell you about Tuesday. Last Tuesday was a very productive day, I left the house. I went and bought groceries."

"Was that the last time you left? Today is Tuesday."

"It's just generally hard to find reasons to even bother these days. I did need to eat though. So, I supposed heading out and down to the store would be an appropriate reason. Come to think of it, I may go again today. It's hard to get myself out there you know, I mean beyond my yard. But all that looking at cake has really made me want a cake, you know? So I'll need to probably go and pick up some supplies for that."

"I really need to talk to you about your bills, Hannah."

"Have you ever made fondant Carla?"

"Wha-? No!"

"Well, neither have I. Guess there's a first time for everything. I ate some off a wedding cake once you know. Absolutely awful taste. But it really doesn't make all those cakes Buddy makes look divine."

"Let's wind this back to-"

"Anyway, thanks for calling but I really must be going. Goodbye Carla." And with that, she abruptly hung up the phone.

With yet another sigh for the day, Carla completed her dance of professional ineptitude and dropped the phone back on the receiver.

"Sighing is not a sound I like to hear, Carla."

She was so caught off guard, she nearly jumped through the ceiling. Whirling around, Arthur stood in her doorway, his stance wide legged. "Arthur! Hi."

He sneezed aggressively into his elbow. "Why don't you come back to my office."

"Oh, okay." She stood up and followed him. People stared as she walked past them, some shrugged and others politely looked at their computer screens. Tim caught her eye, offering her only raised eyebrows and pursed lips on only one side of his face. The pair arrived in Arthur's office. He closed the glass door behind her.

"Oh I tell ya Carla, I really wasn't hoping to have you in here a second time."

"I know Arthur, but things are getting better. I swear."

"You haven't got one skip!" He wheezed. "Carla, you gotta do better."

"I just had a very productive call."

"Naw! Ya didn't!" He squinted his eyes in pain. "Achoo!" He swiped up a tissue out of its holder and violently blew his nose. "You know, this is only gonna get worse. We're headed straight into goldenrod season! What a nightmare."

Carla, normally happy to divert the conversation towards the greener pastures of Arthur's allergies felt she needed to hold her ground. "I swear Ms. Daugherty."

"Ms. Daugherty's file says she's has been outstanding for months."

"But I'm so, so close."

"Carla." Arthur wheezed at her. "I'm sorry, I've gotta write you up."

She sat down into a chair.

"Look, you're a nice kid. But I can't bend the rules for ya. As it is I already held off on the write up. It's going in your employment file."

"Oh God."

"It's not all lost. Get back to that desk and do your job. Got it?" He'd placed both of his hands on his waist in a commanding gesture. She didn't know if he was trying to fool her or himself.

"Right, sure." She stood once again. "Of course." She tried to offer him a better answer but it still came out lamely. She exited his office and Miriam looked at her once again.

"You put money on this too?"

Miriam only shook her head no.

"Well, thanks for that at least." Carla returned to her cubicle and sat down. She wasn't alone for long though. Tim's even keeled footsteps approached her.

"You don't look too happy."

"Correct you are."

"Didn't go well in there, did it?'

"You are two for two, my friend. I got a write up." Under any other circumstances this would've felt like a shameful secret, but she wasn't in the mood to fake anything at the moment.

"You wanna talk about it?"

"Not really. I guess the gist of it is that me and debt collecting once belonged together and now we just don't."

"Sounds like a serious break up."

"Yeap, at first it felt like a pretty easy and natural fit. But I've done it for a while and the original reason I started doing it is kind of gone now. So, I'm not even sure what I'm still doing with it anymore. Debt collection that is."

He let a small laugh escape his lips and looked up. "Well, my boss is roaming into Arthur's office at the moment, so let's do this." He pulled his phone out of his pocket and gave it to Carla. "Throw your number in here and text yourself. If you're ever in the mood to hang out and talk about your debt collection break up… or anything else, let me know."

She stared at the phone for a beat, smiled and took it. She shot a message from his phone to hers and then returned the device to him. "Cool," it was nice of him. "Thanks."

"Totally. I'll catch you later."

Carla watched as he walked away, not knowing what to think about that. She looked down at her phone and saw the message she had sent to herself from his phone. Nico was still in her thoughts. He'd continued to wear her down, but she couldn't let it go. They were fading from one another, but she couldn't throw in the towel and let another week pass by until she heard from him again. She sent him a text to see if he would want to meet up. She spun back around in her chair and looked around at her desk, left with only her thoughts to keep her company.

DAMN YOU

The truth of the matter was that Carla still hadn't been able to bring in a single skip, didn't have the courage to contact Summer, and hadn't kept a single lyric to a single song she had written. Yet she faithfully called Greta and Hannah, continued to study and even mentally draft out what Summer's business plan could look like, and persistently strung together words in her notebook.

She left the calls for the end of each day, and it was through this that her final chat would always be with Hannah. Hannah, unfortunately, would always leave Carla thinking about the one thing. The thing that been mentioned a week ago. Her ghost.

Carla left each day by plugging her head up with ear buds, drowning out the whole world. Normally, she let her iPod surprise her. Today, however, she continued her stroll through Motown with The McCoys' "Hang on Sloopy." It wasn't as though this was a random choice. Reminiscing on being ghosted a second time would only ever bring up one distinct memory. So, as Rick Derringer insisted on Sloopy letting her hair down, Carla crossed over the Longfellow Bridge and thought back to Josie's baby shower.

Her mother had been rushing around the hall they had rented out for it with her hair practically on fire. She haphazardly threw centerpieces on the table as Carla sat stubbornly watching her mother in a tizzy. Josie, roughly the size of an inflated hot air balloon at this point, glided into the room and landed in a chair next to Carla.

"You know, you could get off your ass and help. Look at Mom."

"Well, why don't you float on over there and help her?"

Josie stared at her, incredulous. "I'm pregnant. I'm about to pop."

"You were also the one who insisted on this baby shower, not Mom. No one has more than one baby shower. I've never even heard of that."

"When you have kids, you'll understand."

"No I won't, and no one else does either. You already have all the stuff from Antonietta's baby shower, can't you just reuse that?"

"This is a baby boy in here," she rubbed her stomach.

"So you want to just grease down your relatives and friends for more money? That's nice."

"What the hell is your problem?" she eyed Carla's beverage.

"Go ask your best friend, Paul."

"He's Nick's best friend and you should've thought about that before you two kept going out and breaking up. Watching the both of you is like looking at a car crash."

"Ugh, first of all. He's barely your friend, and even if he was totally your friend, it's been for half a minute. I'm your sister and I have been since forever-"

"Yeah, which is why I told you not to date-"

"-and second of all, we can't keep breaking up. He has seemingly disappeared. Again! Like the fucking Cheshire cat!"

"Oh, have you been dumped? Is that why you're actually like a raging b-"

"Ho no! A respectful adult would've dumped me. This loser has evaporated for the second time now. Can't be bothered to answer a text. Can't be bothered to pick up the phone and call me despite always doing so regularly." She took another elongated sip of wine as their mother continued to whip around them like a whirling dervish.

"I don't understand why you would deal with him for a second time if he ghosted you the first time."

Carla's irritation with both Paul and having to sit through a second baby shower was now even more amplified by the end of her second glass of wine and her sister's inability to just call Paul what he was, an enormous douchebag. "Could we play like, literally any other song right now?"

That day, her sister had glowed red with irritation at her, while her mother tried to keep the production moving along with as much grace as possible.

Carla let the sound of deep moody horns fill her ears as adrenaline earmarked the noises for moments in the future. As Carla arrived at the end of the bridge and the beginning of Cambridge, *Sloopy* was finishing and she hit the pause button. She wished pausing a song could pause her feelings. Unfortunately, they persisted.

She plunked down her bag on the floor of her apartment and whipped out her notepad. She had left her guitar sitting on her bed and she plucked at some random strings to try and get some new sounds bouncing around in her head and the remainder of "Hang on Sloopy" out.

I thought I'd found someone who could reflect
I looked around I was riding alone
He was an ass and I didn't know
I was heading for…

She trailed off, unsure of what she was headed for and so scribbled the words away. They were negative, like before. That must be the problem. Her sunny lyrics from the top of the page had been morphed into beleaguered and downtrodden. This wasn't the song she wanted to sing. But those were the feelings that were coming to her now.

She set the words to one side and looked at her phone once more. After one week of radio silence and a now an unanswered text for two more days, Carla was feeling something a little different from the despair she'd forged in her notebook. It was frustration. She recognized the hollow pit in her gut, the kind where a realization had previously come to her far more slowly, but the muscle memory took hold. She looked distrustfully at the phone now. It was the purveyor of this unwelcome piece of information.

Carla chose to believe that she was wrong and that she would get an answer, and that this answer would include an apology for being so distant. Nico walked around with a phone that was essentially affixed to hand. Did he all of a sudden drop it in a toilet? Must she be so disrespected yet another time by yet another guy?

She tried to distract herself once again by plucking at some more strings on her guitar, but nearly shot through the roof when her phone's buzzer sent vibrations through her mattress. It was, however, not Nico, but Jas, wanting to know if she would come by at some point to work on their song for the song contest. She replied with a quick, *yeah, sure, whenever you want,* and returned to moping about.

One more vibration went through her phone and she looked back down at it, expecting to see yet another text from Jas, but found herself surprised. It was Summer, and she wanted to come over. Carla wasn't in the mood for people, but she had been beyond absent lately and so accepted.

Not long thereafter, she heard a knock on her door. When Carla opened it, Summer stood there before her. It felt strange in a way it never had before. "Hi."

"Hey."

Never in their time since they were small, even at their first meeting, had Summer's presence ever felt akin to that of a stranger. A stilted silence now hung in the air between them as two friends who hadn't spoken much in quite a while confronted each other.

"You want to come in? I have vodka." Not great first words to have for an estranged best friend, but the words were all she had in her mind, and emergency guest vodka was all she had in her freezer.

"I guess so."

"Cool." Carla produced two mugs from her cabinet and set them down on the counter. She cracked cubes out of her ice tray and poured the vodka over them. Her fridge was devoid of mixers though. "Is on the rocks okay? Sorry. It's just I didn't realize you were coming and I don't have anything."

"It's all good. I'm the person you used to help steal Arlo's Wonderballs as a kid, not like a foreign dignitary. We regularly drink wine out juice glasses at the Purple Salmon."

This got Carla to crack a smile. "Touché."

The two friends sat down, Carla on her bed while Summer occupied the chair and continued on with their trend of silence.

"Maybe we take a drink first?"

"Yeah, yeah. Good plan."

"Okay, I know I have to start. I know why you came by."

"I mean the fact we just stared at each other weirdly for, like, five minutes pretty much says it all."

"I know I haven't been around much."

"Yeah."

"It isn't that I'm wanting to blow you off."

"But you have blown me off and I know Jas spoke with you."

"You do?" Carla sipped her vodka more.

"Yeah," Summer followed suit. "There are a million bars in Cambridge but for some reason we all only go to one, and eventually everyone knows your name, you know?"

"True, true."

"I know he went to tell you to hang out with me. But here's the thing, don't hang out with me if you need to be told to. I don't know why you fell off the radar. I mean I'm guessing it's Nico."

"Only sort of."

"Well, whatever. But the point is, we've been like sisters always. More than you and Josie ever and I guess what I don't get is where you've gone and why my husband has to be the one to tell you to reach out once in a while."

"Life just gets clogged up with stuff. Nothing is fun right now. I know that isn't an excuse for anything Summer, I'm sorry. I'm really, really sorry."

"Clogged up with what?"

"Just stuff, and yeah, like you said about the Nico thing, I do feel like it's a little bit him, but not entirely. I'd be lying if I said that. Honestly, it's, it's work."

"No one likes their job."

"I'm starting to think some people might. This guy, Tim, at my work is in accounting and appears to enjoy it."

"Oh… gross."

"I know right? But anyway." She adjusted her sitting position and drank more vodka as the words became increasingly forthcoming with each sip. "I lost track of what I was doing there."

"You mean making money so that you could like pay rent and utilities and eat and stuff?"

"I mean, I didn't want to have a bunch of student debt and now I don't, but I paid that off a while ago. Once I paid it off, I slowly just stopped doing well at work. For a while it was cool to have the money rolling in like that, but I've lived like this," she motioned to her tiny speck of apartment, "for a long time now. I throw my money in the bank and that's it. It all sits there. I don't know what I'm doing."

"What do you want to do?"

"Not call people in debt with no way out all day and grease them for money they don't have."

"So get a different job?"

"I don't know what. And I've got cash laying around, and so what if I make more? You know? I mean, I've never felt safe in my life that way before, but once I started to, I started thinking about what I really wanted. This is it? For the next whatever years of my life?"

"Okay. So, get a different job."

"I don't know if I'll be good at any job anymore. I'm not even good at collecting debt anymore. I've been sucking at it for a while now."

"Oh."

"What if I lose it?"

"Lose what?"

"My job."

"Is it really that bad?" Summer sipped more, now entranced.

"I could live for a while, but definitely not forever and yeah, it's that bad." Carla's looked down at her glass.

"I got written up for…" she wasn't really sure the exact terminology. "I dunno. For sucking I guess?" She cracked a genuine smile at this and Summer followed suit. The two girls laughed with one another for the first time in months. "Oh my," she honked between her laughs, "I'm so screwed."

"Arlo was like that, you know?"

"Huh?"

"Yeah, it's why he went to L.A."

"I thought he and Devin just wanted to get out of here."

"Naw. Well, I mean, kinda. He thought he was drowning here. He didn't care about this bookstore. He hit a point, but you know, like, years before now, where he needed to change everything. He was afraid that if he didn't, he wouldn't change anything."

"Shit."

"Yeah, well, it worked out. It's just him and Devin and their dog, Sammy."

"I spose, yeah." Carla looked up again. "What about you?"

"What do you mean?"

"You don't know what's going on in my life. I don't know what's going on in yours."

Summer leaned back in her chair. "I'm spinning my wheels."

"What do you mean?"

"You know how you said all that stuff about making a case and coming up with a business plan?"

"Yeah?"

"It's been a stretch for me."

"What do you mean?"

"It's just a lot, I keep getting stuck on some parts."

"You'll get it, though."

"Naw, not with that and keeping up with regular hours of work and trying to have a life and stuff."

"It's your side hustle."

"I know, but side hustles are hard."

Carla looked at her raised eyebrows. "Here," she held up her mug, "with me now. Here's to our jobs sucking and our side hustles being not so hustle-y-ish. Whatever. Just chug it with me." They both threw back the remainder of what was in their mugs. The liquid choked them both back. "Summer."

"Yes, Carla."

"You are the one who takes stabs at things. You can't be down on yourself because you get it done. I'm not a cheerleader."

"I'd agree, based on this pep talk."

"But! You are good at pushing people around you, and I think you've got this and I think you've got a good idea. Now," she let out a disgusting, juicy belch.

"Ew, now what?"

"Let's go watch the planes land."

"It's getting dark out."

"You have your car!"

"And a belly full of vodka," she giggled back at her.

"I will call an Uber!"

"Well, if you insist."

Carla located the appropriate app on her phone and summoned a car. She looked around at Summer, who was still perched on her chair. "One more shot before we go?"

"Ehhh, may as well."

"Here we go."

The two threw back their shots, though once again out of coffee mugs and walked down and into their car. Carla had been afraid of the alcohol wearing off by the time they made it to Winthrop, but the restorative shot had safely carried their buzz through to the beach.

The pair got out of the car and a confused and suspicious driver flew down the street away from them.

The planes were landing on the right runway that afternoon. Sometimes, as teenagers, the girls would come down to the seaside by the very spot Carla and her father would inhabit when she was small, but they didn't always hit it quite right. The planes had to be landing on the correct runway or the trip was all for naught. Carla and Summer sat down on a seawall and looked down at the rocks that lay bare, as the tide was out. Across the bay sat the city, and to their backs was a line of cape style houses with carefully manicured lawns and frequently replaced roofs. The sun was slowly saying goodbye to the day. It hadn't sunk down fully into night, but it was hidden behind the skyscrapers of Boston.

"Hear it?" Summer asked. "I think one is on its way."

The rumble came in from behind them, the sound gradually growing louder. They looked up to the sky and a green-bellied plane flew over their heads. It was so close, Carla could've sworn she could reach up and touch it. The Aer Lingus plane continued on for a smooth landing, leaving a blanket of brown smog in its wake.

"Wonder what they all got up to wherever they were."

"What? In Ireland?"

"Well, yeah, I 'spose there's a good chance they were in Ireland."

"Probably just a bunch of tourists running up to that stone and kissing it."

"I heard locals pee on that stone."

"Yeah, probably."

"I mean if we, as a city, had a stone like that, I bet people would be peeing left and right on it."

"True story. We haven't been here in… I don't even know how long," Summer balanced her body weight on her arms. "Feels like forever."

"I miss it. You know? Down by the sea. It just feels good here, like you can breathe. And, the planes are nice, 'cause you never know where anything is coming or going from… well, I mean unless the plane is huge and green and has a huge shamrock on it I s'pose."

"Anything else going on?"

Carla looked over at Summer. She'd been hoping to avoid talking about the cliché of her dating life. Mainly, the bit where she'd disappeared in part because of it. "It's Nico." She was getting tired of even thinking of his stupid name. "Something feels just, not right, you know?"

"No. But, to be honest, this whole Nico person is pretty mysterious. I mean other than when I saw him. He isn't literally mysterious. Actually, he's pretty basic in a hipster-esque kind of way."

"See? You don't even actually know him, but you've managed to figure that out."

"What isn't quite right?"

"I know you don't want to hear this, but it feels kinda Paul-ish."

"Dude, you can't use him as a benchmark for, like, everyone you date."

"I don't!"

"Yeah, you do. Every time you go out with someone you find something remotely related to something Paul once did and end it."

"Can you blame me? You know the absolute nightmare that whole sorry episode ended with."

"I think we can safely blame that on your antics."

"Yeah, but I was needled to the point of extremism."

"Well, I think we can say at the least it provided rooms number two-twenty-two through two forty-five at the Sonesta with quite a bit of entertainment… at like two in the morning or whatever."

"It's the fade."

"What's that mean?"

"I can feel the slow slide off, I know it's coming. The fade off is in effect, I swear."

"Naw. Did you contact him? Sometimes you can be a little… aloof."

"Aloof."

"Yeah, I don't mean that in a bad way. I mean like you're a very guarded person. Sometimes. Sorta."

"I don't see how that's getting any better."

"Did you try reaching out to him? You don't do that sometimes. Your words, not mine."

"More like Paul's accusations."

"Ugh, see? You did it again. Stop living by the stuff he said. He played head games."

"And yes, for your information, I did."

"If that's the case and he's planning on doing the fade to black move, then I can't see why you'd feel all that bad anyway; the kid's missing out."

Carla looked over at Summer. "Thanks. I'm lucky your mom and dad decided to move in next door when we were, like, six."

"I *know*, right?" Summer mockingly winked at her. "Wanna just stand up and do what we came to do?"

"Yes 'mam."

They stood up and Carla looked over at Summer, "You're gonna get your business plan and I'm gonna sort out everything at work. We got this." She looked up at the rumble in the sky. "Ready?"

"Most definitely."

As plane grew closer, their adrenaline and liquid courage intertwined and crawled through their veins. They looked up and the nose of the plane crept into view. No one could hear anything besides fuel being shot out of engines in a hot, fiery blast. They filled their lungs with air and screamed. They screamed out frustrations, misfortunes, and uncertainty. They screamed to release their fear. Eventually, the air died out of their lungs and the plane sped away from them, towards its final destination on the runway. They stood in silence a moment longer, until Summer's voice cut in, "That felt good."

"Yeah, I think we needed that." Carla felt the words leave her body. "I'll call the Uber home?"

"Yeah, I think it's time to go home." She navigated her way through her phone to an Uber and a car navigated its way to them.

Soon enough, they were back at Carla's, exiting the sedan that had transported them back to Cambridge. Summer looked back at Carla, "No more disappearing acts?"

"No more, promise!"

"Jas and his band are meeting up tomorrow night, should I tell him you'll be there?"

"Hundred percent. I'll head there after work."

"And don't let work get you down, okay?"

"Got it, don't let the bookstore get you down, okay?"

"Yes mam," she walked to her car and looked back. "Don't let that Nico get you down either."

"Never."

Summer sat down in her car, cranked over the engine and sped away. Carla turned and walked up stairs. It was hot and stuffy inside compared to the crispness of the night outside. The windiness of the sea had left her arms wind burnt, only bringing her temperature up even more.

She ripped of her pants, unable to take the heat any more. She donned the tank top that she slept in and wanted to just collapse on her bed. It could've been the screaming, or maybe the inhalation of airplane exhaust fumes, or just the leftover vodka that persisted, locked into her veins, but Carla couldn't lay down. She wasn't ready. She needed to move. She needed another shot. She helped herself. The people one unit up made enough noise, so why couldn't she?

The screaming had been good, but singing could be even better, so it would be The Who's "You Better You Bet" that would take her truly home that night. It was the first finger picks on Roger Daltry's guitar that plugged her into the songs. It was the first few declarations of "you better you bets" that made her swing her hips around. She grabbed at the continually emptying bottle of vodka and sang passionately into it. Every pronunciation of "you bet" boosted her up. She could feel the hard backbone of percussion pulsing up and down her spine; she could stomp her feet and jump up and down, and that made perfect sense. She was perfectly in time with the beat. It was the final demands made towards the end of the song that queued her to drop to her knees in true rock star form and aggressively sing out to the heavens that someone better love her all the time and that they better shove her back into line. But, it was really the guitar solo that possessed her and lifted her back to a stand. She skated on her bare feet through her postage stamp apartment and half-head banged-half screamed her way through that final verse. It was back to a haphazard hop for her last moments making love to that song and it was a careful collapse onto her back, onto her bed for the final words, which she said to her ceiling.

Carla didn't care to listen to anything else for the rest of her night. The knocking on her door went ignored, and the ignored finally went away. Her eyes slid shut, through the alcohol and through the sound of the people up stairs and through her own ceiling light that glared down meanly at her. All was dark; eventually, all was quiet.

Carla sat behind her desk and punched at the various buttons on the screen of her iPhone. The morning had been a real slap in the face and a hangover had followed her into work, haunting her like a ghost. Sleeping on her back with her legs flopped out of bed hadn't been a particularly dignified choice nor a comfortable one. She reached around and massaged the muscles at the nape of her neck. Today wasn't going fast enough.

The previous night had felt good. Summer had jumped the hurdle she had needed to, but their friendship felt back to normal. She still hadn't heard from Nico, but she tried to remember what Summer had said last night and what Jas had told her even before that. There was, of course, still the more pressing matter surrounding her newfound ineptitude at her job as well as her inability to string two verses together in a song. She knew she was meant to come up with something. Practice was tonight; she'd promised him, she'd promised Summer, and she'd promised herself that she would go.

Being at that practice with Jas seemed more important than listening to Hannah Daugherty go through her daily chores. She set her pen to yet another blank page of her notepad and some more words streamed out of her.

My friends reach out and they buzz me
But im tired I hope theyll leave
The ships gone down I just need a nap

These were better than the last ones; at least they weren't disingenuous. They were ugly though. She re-read them several times. Things weren't sunny, she allowed the creeping fear of paranoia to wash over her frequently, and nothing felt as cool as she had written it. She wasn't writing how she felt, she was writing how she wanted to feel. The lyrics weren't as sloppy as Carla was in life. But she didn't want the world to see the absolute mess that was her mind.

Knuckles were coming into repeated contact with the felt of a cubical wall. "Can I interrupt?"

"I s'pose if you must." She swiveled to see Tim relaxed coolly against the doorway to her cube. Or at least as coolly as one could in an ill-fitting button down and what her mother would probably refer to as *slacks*.

"The sneezer in chief seems to have left the

building."

"Thank God for that. He's been up my ass lately." She felt it prudent to leave out the part about it being because she was sucking at her job lately.

"Yeah, I've noticed." He cranked his head to one side, taking a clear aim to see what Carla had been doodling. "So whatcha been doing? Definitely isn't work." He smirked at the pad.

She swiveled in her chair back and forth trying to obstruct his view of her words. "Just some lyrics."

"You're a singer?"

"More a songwriter, but you kinda have to sing them before anyone else can I guess?"

"That's cool."

"Thanks."

"So like, where's my song?"

"Uhmm…" She stared at him, unsure if he'd been joking.

"Jeez, chill out. I'm messing with you."

"Oh," she guffawed back out at him, relaxed. "Right, of course."

"I was actually wondering if you wanted to go out."

That made her spine sharpen up like a stick. "Oh, yeah. Totally." She'd been caught off-guard and much to her own dismay she was reflexively agreeable.

"Awesome. Yeah, you around anytime in particular?"

"Just text me. I live in Cambridge so I'm pretty much always around all weekend, so, yeah. Anytime, really." Why did she always have to speak so many words?

"Cool," he stood up off the doorway of her cube in a motion to leave. "So I'll se you this weekend."

"Totally."

He started walking away, "Better have my song ready for me."

"Right," she laughed, causing her to loosen once

again.

That should have been something to look forward to. But it wasn't. She stared at her stupid song that wasn't even a song yet and her eyes looked over to her stupid phone. The previous night and all the resolve it was meant to bring her was melting away.

She hadn't been able to think about work to begin with, but now her song seemed even more out of reach. She hadn't been wanting anything one way or another with Tim, yet the opportunity presented itself. She wanted to claim she didn't want anything with Nico one way or another, yet the need for a response lingered. She thought back to his lectures about turtles and his stupid red suspenders, and most angrily, the time he'd told her it was smart of her to leave school and her music. But she wanted to see him despite all that. So that maybe, one last time, if she did, he would be nice. She just needed this one time, this person she'd listened to and given advice to, to show her kindness.

She sent Arthur an e-mail, feigning illness and ducked out of work early, once again. It was while she was walking over the Longfellow Bridge in the boiling summer sun that she would receive a text. It was short and to the point.

Sorry. Haven't been around. People from out of town visiting.

There were many things Carla had tolerated, some a predicament that life had landed her in and others, trifles that were entirely of her own making. She had seen this particular trifle once before; she would not allow for it again. Though the walk home was long, her feet propelled her forward, anger being the fuel source. Sloppily written excuses were only ever followed by radio silence. She would not let someone else have the final word a second time. Never again.

Carla paced around her studio. The emergency vodka she'd stashed in her freezer for company was looking considerably lower. She looked back at the sloppy words he had texted to her earlier. They burned through the touchscreen glass and seared into her forehead. They carved their way through to her mind. She took another swig from the bottle. She was furious. Why build her up, Buttercup? The stupid song echoed through her mind and back to the day she angrily sat next to her apathetic, pregnant lard ball of a sister. This wouldn't happen again. Not to her, not with some other imbecile. She would never live through another Paul. She would never give anyone else a second, even third chance. The days of a soppy, drunken mess of a sad Carla were gone. A furious, fully loaded, spiteful Carla had emerged. She reviewed the skeleton of her life; she had pushed away her friends, been royally failing to do her job and now she had this self-involved, spoiled brat of a human dumping on her to her face and quietly fading into the background.

She didn't even like Nico at this point, and she wouldn't stand for it if he ghosted her in the same way as Paul. So she carefully balanced her phone in her hands and sat on her bed. She would begin with a text, she decided. No. That wouldn't be impactful enough, would it? A phone call it would be. She didn't even talk on the phone outside of her skip traces. She never called her sister or Summer or Jas. But on this occasion, she would happily make an exception.

"Here we go. You call me all the Goddamn time and you know what? I would go over. I would schlep over to your apartment and I would sit there. I would sit and I would listen. Over the course of our time together I listened to you piss and moan about your parents and your band mates and your stupid brother, who, by the way, you think is the lesser favored of the two you, but let's be honest, one of you stuck at home has a stable girlfriend and is on your way to being a doctor and the other is a self-righteous quote on quote *artist* who has some bullshit boat tattooed on his arm and is a sieve for their money. So, nice try on that one. Oh, and by the way-"

She halted. The phone cut her off. Crap. She'd have to call back again. She ran the risk having to actually speak to him if he picked up. She remembered, however, that he wouldn't pick up ever because of the many things in life Carla wasn't certain of. She definitely knew when she was being ghosted. She redialed, getting more annoyed at each buzzing tone.

"As I was saying. By the way, your stupid tattoo isn't fucking new or original; you'll probably never get anchored down because you're a miserable shit. But, that isn't the point of this call. The point of this call is to let you know that if you didn't want this to be a thing, then the deal is, we hook up and then we move on. I don't care about your problems, I don't care about your dreams, I don't need to waste my time giving you advice and making you feel better about yourself you fucking narcissi-"

The phone gave another loud and piercing beep as her voicemail was cut off for a second time. She was really getting tired of getting cut off in phone conversations. *Even the phone calls between me and a machine won't let me get all my words out.* "Alright, one last time."

"Just so you know, your suspenders are dumb. The fact that you think I've never felt loss is bullshit, and no one in the history of planet earth ever wanted to hear The Beatles played on bongos you hack. I'd tell you to lose my number, but just to make sure, I'm gonna lose yours first. You self-involved, elitist, piece of shit. Goodbye."

She sat back down on her bed with shaky arms once more and looked down in horror at her phone. She hit the red, end-call button, victorious, and continued to stare at the phone as though it was a foreign object. *What did I just do?* Those were words that were never good to have run through your mind. Indeed, what had she done?

She let years of frustration with her life and months of frustration with him bubble up. Her thoughts were baking soda, and the vodka she had drenched herself in was the vinegar. The mess was living in Nico's inbox. Paul had always had the final say in everything, but Nico would not.

Carla believed that the likelihood he would attempt to make any sort of remote contact with her was somewhere in the realm of zero percent, but through her forever increasing drunken stupor, she somehow found a way to giggle at the remains of this mess of a night. She wasn't proud of her behavior, but it felt like she had scaled a mountain she previously had rolled down several times. *And who would've thought,* she continued to reason with herself, *all it took was one loud, screaming drunk-dial.*

Carla's self-congratulatory state would be short-lived, as it happened. She collapsed back on her bed, still elated from the intoxicating combination of booze and an ejection of feelings. *No wonder people went to therapy,* she began on a new train of thought before a knock on the door interrupted her. She lifted her head and stared at the door. The knock persisted, even louder than before. *Shit.* She must've angered her neighbors with her shouting. She hadn't realized how loud she had become, her volume increasing slowly to a scream.

Carla made her way to the door and wretched it open. Rather than an agitated neighbor, she found a disapproving Summer followed by a disappointed Jas. The two silently marched in to her studio. Carla's sass evaporated.

"Hi. Nice to see you. I'm your long lost best friend. Maybe you remember me? Name's Summer." She stuck out a hand.

"Sum, don't be dramatic." Jas stood farther in the background.

"Don't tell me not to be dramatic." She looked straight at Carla, "You totally left him hanging tonight."

"I'm sorry."

"And you've left us both hanging for a while."

"I know, I'm sorry!" Carla threw up her hands. "God! Just give me a break okay? I've got stuff going on right now."

"Yeah, you smell like it."

"Oh go to hell."

"Hey, hey!"

"No. Not 'hey!' We went and watched the planes together; we talked about this."

"I know." Carla was feeling more and more sober by the minute. "I'm sorry, I know we screamed it out. It was just that then all this stuff happened."

"Yeah, we did scream it out. I thought after everything we said, this disappearing act you keep pulling would be over. It's unfair. I don't know what the hell could be going on in your life that's so terrible that you have to completely ditch your friends. Is it all because of some douchebag guy?"

"No!"

"Well, what is it? Cause I thought we had talked it out and that I could just have my friend back after this, but apparently we didn't."

"Well, the douchebag guy is gone now. Okay? Pretty sure I just drove him off for good if that does anything to make you feel better."

"Well then, what? What is it?"

Carla looked at the two of them standing before her. She was tired; it had been a full day and she couldn't do another night like the airplane night yet again. "You know what? We already did this whole conversation."

"Yeah, and at the end of it you said you'd turn it around and get back on track."

"I'm trying! I'm getting there!"

"You aren't trying hard enough."

"Carla," Jas piped up through his meditative silence. "I don't ask for much and to be honest, I invited you to this contest 'cause I thought it'd be fun and I thought it would've been good for you. We all have our shit. You don't like your man? Don't see him anymore-"

"-Well, actually-"

"-You don't like your job? Welcome to the club. No one does, but we all have them."

"I know that."

"You want to be a song writer, musician, singer, whatever. Well, come and join me. But you didn't, you blew me off. Again." He shook his head. "I don't need to go on and on about this. You either show up and care or just exist. Those are your choices in life. Everyone has their pile of crap in life to deal with. I guess some of us in life deal with it better than others."

"Jas, I'm sorry, I'm sorry, I'm sorry." It wasn't a lie, "I swear."

"Doesn't really matter right now does it? You know where we hang and where I practice. So show up or don't. It's up to you."

"I'm sorry."

"I'm pretty over hearing you say that. Jas talked to you and then I did. I thought we were beyond this. We screamed at the planes! I guess we aren't though."

"We are, I swear! I needed one day."

"It's always one day." Summer started walking back to the door. "Just so you know, I'm here telling you this now so you've been informed that the way you've been acting is bullshit."

"So what?" Carla said, "Is that it?"

"Yeah, that's it, we figured if we didn't show up in person, we may never hear from you again." The pair left her almost as quickly as they had arrived. Carla watched as Jas closed the door behind him. Her feelings of triumph had been fleeting and now she was left alone, relegated once again to muddling around in disappointment.

DOLEDRUM

Carla dragged one foot in front of the other into work. She'd somehow managed to eliminate three people from her life in one fell swoop. She had also arrived for the second day in a row with quite the hangover. It currently felt like pins were playing ping pong against the inside of her skull.

She sat down behind her desk and started up her old clunker of a computer. The lights were glaring down at her, disapprovingly. The computer screen produced a beautiful image filled with the saccharine colors of Monterey Bay. Why did they always have to tease you? Auto programmed desktop computers could be cruelest creatures on earth. It was enough of a slap in the face that you were trapped inside all day, caged like an animal, but then, they had the audacity to show you an image of some other gorgeous place you'd rather be.

It was already ten in the morning, far too late a start than she'd meant. She figured she may as well start with Greta, see whatever new collagen induced product had hit the market today. Her intent was for not, though, as soft padded footsteps came in behind her.

"You can't be expecting an entire song to be finished already," she said the words as she swiveled, only to realize that the man she expected to be Tim was in fact Arthur.

"That's quite the gesture, Carla, but I really didn't have it on my radar."

"Oh, Arthur, I'm sorry. It was just I-"

"Why don't you come with me, Carla." He let out a long wheeze.

"Sure, Arthur."

The lack of information didn't sit well with Carla. The fact that these visits from Arthur were increasing didn't either. As she followed him into his office, Miriam didn't even make eye contact. Sometimes it wasn't a person's words that sent the loudest message, but a complete lack thereof.

He plodded around behind his desk, simultaneously grabbing a tissue and sitting down. Carla stood opposite him. He violently sneezed and then looked up at her.

"Why don't you sit down?"

"I'm fine."

He motioned wildly at her. "Please! Achoo! Ah Jesus, I'll tell ya."

Carla sank into the chair, still nervous for what she thought would be undoubtedly yet another verbal lashing. One even she, herself, would admit was deserved. She was poised and ready to take it, but she was also wrong. No drawn out lectures could be directed toward her, instead there were only a few simple words that Arthur had for her.

"Carla, I have to fire you."

"Arthur?" It came out as a question, because she wasn't entirely sure what he meant by those words. She knew what they meant, but it had never occurred to her that they would be presented to her.

"I'm sorry, Carla." He grabbed another tissue and sneezed even harder. She was certain one of these day he would bust a blood vessel. "Ahh Jesus. I'm sorry I can't even just fire you right. These allergies, I tell ya."

"It's fine." Her head was a balloon floating somewhere a few feet above her body. She wasn't speaking so much as listening to herself talk. It wasn't fine though, so why had she said so? "I just thought I could turn it around. You know?"

"I know you did, but your head hasn't been in the game for a while now."

"I could still do better." Her eyelids were heavy and it occurred to her that she should have been white hot with anxiety. All her security was gone. Everything she had given up was for nothing. The tally of things lost had gone from three people to three people and a job. She was just tired. All she wanted was to go home and sleep.

"It's too late Carla, we keep numbers; eventually the numbers catch up with you, and you haven't been pulling in the money you used to for a while. It's out of my hands."

She couldn't even summon the energy to argue with him. "Should I clear out my desk?"

"I'll come with you. I need to take your laptop. You can leave your badge with me."

"Oh, okay." As they stood and walked and returned to her desk, Carla popped the laptop out of the port and handed it over to Arthur. She unclipped the badge from her polyester pants. *No,* she thought, *I haven't lost three people and a job. I lost three people, and a job I took to pay back what I owed for my music.* So, what had it all been for? She grabbed the doodle notebook and Arthur motioned to the elevator. They walked over to it and she was confused as Arthur followed her in. Carla looked at him, a question written across her face.

"Achoo!" He erupted in yet another sneeze. "Ugh, Jesus. I'm sorry. It's just protocol, I have to escort you out of the building."

"But what would I-"

"I know you've got nothing on you. It just something I have to do. As a manager."

And that was the state of affairs. No music, no guy, no friends, no job, and she had to be escorted out of the building like a criminal.

It was actually a gorgeous day out, which made it all that much worse. She paused over the Longfellow Bridge. The sky was clear and went for miles. The sun warmed her skin but it wasn't too hot. The river caught specks of light and it sparkled back up at Carla. She didn't care. She looked down at the sailboats being operated by people in the beginning stages of learning how to use them. One tipped over, but that didn't even bring her much amusement, so she continued on her journey into Cambridge though home wasn't her particular direction. She didn't know in particular where she was even walking, but ultimately, and unsurprisingly, her feet brought her to The Purple Salmon.

The sleep hadn't worn off her yet, but at least inside the dingy bar, her eyes could open a little more fully. She perched herself on a bar stool and called over to the bartender. She didn't recognize this tall, heavily bearded man. Then again, she'd been at her desk job during this time for nearly a decade.

"What can I do ya for?" he rumbled jovially at her.

She really wanted to make an overdramatic pun at him. A new lease on life perhaps? A time machine that would make all choices leading up to now disappear? Some fairy dust so that all her troubles could evaporate? "Vodka on the rocks'd work," was all that came out. She figured hair of the dog would be her best bet. If there wasn't a better time to day drink alone when you got fired, then when would there be?

A glass of ice and what she knew to be clear, liquid fire appeared before her. She tasted the poison and tried not to scrunch her face into a cringed up little ball. Ordering alcohol you couldn't actually handle drinking wasn't a good look. While she didn't care about much at the moment, she did care about that. Aside from the vodka was the present issue of money. Sure, she had saved money over the years. As soon as she'd received her first paycheck, she had savored it. The only thing she found more satisfying than that was the first paycheck she could keep for herself. She'd have her rent to pay and food to eat, but when her student loans had been whittled down to nothing, there was nothing greater than looking in her bank account and seeing actual money. For the first time in her life, she felt like she really had something. The feeling of missing out on school and spending her days inside a cave wearing people down until they succumbed to payment plans had been worth it.

Now though, what would she do? She had a bank full of money but what would she spend it on? Absolutely nothing. She could subsist on very little for quite a while. But, to have given up so much for financial security only to then obliterate it was painful. She wondered once again what was left for her at the moment. She closed her eyes and threw back everything she could in the glass and beckoned to the bartender.

"Can I have another one…"

"Phil."

"Phil! Can I have another one, Phil?"

"Sure can." He went about pouring her another round.

"Thanks."

"Are you okay?"

"Hah," she nearly snorted in his face. "Do you have any magic ways I can earn a regular paycheck?"

"Bartender."

"That's cheating."

"But it's still a way to earn a living."

"Okay, fair Phil, I'll give you that one. Got any openings?"

"Negative."

"Any other suggestions?" She took a sip, again trying not to cringe.

"My cousin makes bank off being a dog walker."

"Seriously?"

"Yeah, you know how many tech nerds live in Davis Square and don't wanna walk their own dogs? Like, a lot."

"How'd he get them, flyers? I mean I like dogs and walking and money."

"I think it was mainly word of mouth."

"Oh, that won't work then. I don't even have one mouth."

"Rover."

"What does that mean?"

"Or Wag or something. You could do that. They're apps."

Carla continued to sip; the distraction of dog walking apps was welcome. "Okay," she pulled out her phone. "Wag." She said the words as she typed them in.

Sure enough, a cheery little icon with an exclamation point appeared before her. *Okay*, she thought, *this could work*. She started checking through all the questions. *I could make dog walking money and this, everything I've done in my life, wouldn't be a waste. I just need to be a dog walker*. She took another sip and saw that Wag! was requesting a reference or two to corroborate the existence of the imaginary dogs she had claimed to own. Crap. She assumed Summer and Jas were out on that front. Which momentarily made her eyes cast downward as she imagined how fun it would have been to at least be able to laugh about her future as a dog walker with Summer. She'd have to go with plan B.

Hey Josie
What do you want?
I need you tell Wag! That I've owned dogs.
That's what you have to say to me?
Yeah I really need this right now
You're such an ass
Please? Seriously I need this
Seriously?

She could feel Josie's eyes rolling back in her head right now.

What the hell is Wag!
A dog walking app
Why
Can you just do it? I really need you to
Fine!
Thanks
Whatever

Carla continued sipping and tried not to think about Summer. But, the more she tried not to think at all, the more she wound up thinking. Her eyes had begun to burn as she reflected on the friends she'd let down, the boss she'd let down, and most of all, how she had let herself down. Her cheeks had begun sizzling as her emotions were ready and rearing to take hold. She was saved by the bell though. Clearly, Josie had come through for her and she was on to the dog safety portion of the quiz.

Phil meandered back over from the far end of the bar. "You all good?"

"I need another."

"On it."

"Hey Phil, do you know anything about dog safety?"

"Absolutely not."

"Oh, cool, great."

How bad could this be? Google is a thing. I'll just Google the answers. Some nerd probably put them all on Reddit anyway.

Phil placed her third vodka in front of her and she took a slug from it almost immediately. "I'm gonna take a quiz on dog safety now," she announced to Phil.

"Go get 'em tiger."

The first few questions were about leashes, so that hadn't seemed so bad. Some of the photos were a little hard to find, especially as she was having to navigate between apps so much. The even trickier ones were surrounding what to do if dogs were trying to fight each other or if they ran away from you or if their tails were pointing downward. But, again, she felt reasonably okay with the grand majority of the stolen answers she'd found. She took one more giant slug from her glass, victorious.

Phil had taken a break from looking at the television to look back at her.

"Well Phil-"

"You really don't have to keep saying my name."

"-this is the first day of the rest of my life."

"As a dog walker?"

"Yes, Phil. Yes." She triumphantly hit "submit."

"Okay," he shrugged.

She continued to sip and forced her mind to stay focused on dogs. Everyone liked dogs. Dogs are furry and you can pet them, they're always happy to see you and they never tell you they would love to hang out with you, but then never respond to texts in a timely fashion. A dog would never do that. A cat would maybe, but definitely not a dog. Nico was totally a cat.

Her phone violently vibrated at her making her pop up on her bar stool.

"Wow there Sparky, you wanna chill out a little bit?"

"My name is Carla!" She opened her email and saw Wag! They were undoubtedly replying to her to let her know that they would love it if she would walk as many dogs as possible. At least she believed so until she read the contents of said email.

"Okay *Carla*."

"Oh my God."

"Yes *Carla*?"

Carla, finally, was done. She was cooked. Her eyes had begun to sting once more and she could feel the heat burning off of her cheekbones. If it was at all possible for steam to emanate from a person's skull in a bar that currently sat in a tepid state, this would have been that moment. A big fat blob of a tear burst from her eye and rolled down her face with increasing speed. It curled under her jawbone, clinging to her skin for dear life. "Phil," she choked on the words. "I'm never gonna do it."

"What?" His face was recoiling into a look of horror as he realized what was happening.

"I'm never gonna be a dog walker."

"You seem to be taking it a bit hard."

A horrible guttural sob emerged from her throat. "Over the course of my summer I have dated a man who was a grade A asshole and somehow I still managed to hang on to the point where he ghosted me, I ditched out on my friends and now they won't deal with me, I haven't written one coherent word of a song, I've lost my will to collect debt so my boss had to fire me, and now look at me!" Her voice had slowly made its way from a muddled stutter to an all out scream. "I was rejected from being a dog walker. The powers that be have decided that I am unfit for walking dogs!"

"It seems like you have a lot going on."

"I do, I really, really do, Phil." She sucked down the last of her drink.

"That's tough."

"Can I work here? I need a job," she choked the request out.

"Based on this performance, I'd say no."

"Oh." She wiped away the tears. "Yeah, that's fair, that's fair."

"Could I call you a cab?"

"No, I live nearby. Aren't you supposed to have more helpful words here?"

"I'm a bartender, not a therapist. I've also already used up my lines."

"No more lines for me?"

"That'll be thirty even please."

"Fine." She whipped out her wallet and threw down the cash. "You don't care about me, Phil. So, I'll just go."

"Thank you?"

With that, Carla slinked unevenly off her stool and ran back outside, vowing to never go back to The Purple Salmon at the same time of day ever again lest Phil remember that horrific display. And really, how could he not?

Carla had a few dearly held beliefs about music. One was that she determined everyone's brain grew differently, so it stood to reason that while some people felt a euphoria unlike any other when they ate a bite of food or had a drink of alcohol, that a certain pleasure center in their brain was hit. Hers must have been the hearing part of her brain. Another, more song specific belief would have to be that no matter how many new bands she heard and jived with, the older ones would always be better.

It was this thought that ran through her head presently as she stood outside The Purple Salmon while The Temptations' "Ain't Too Proud To Beg" blared through the outdoor speakers, and also in her past the last time she'd heard that song. It was, unfortunately, at yet another wedding. A relative of her brother-in-law's to be exact. She hadn't wanted to go, but after Josie married herself to Nick, this meant that Carla was married to his whole family apparently.

So as drunk bridesmaids swirled their way around the dance floor stuffed like sausages into taupe taffeta, Carla tried to keep a low profile at her own table in the rear corner. In-laws may have been invited, but they weren't given priority seating, thankfully. She sipped on the free prosecco that was being dutifully refilled by the wait staff. It was her beverage of choice should her mother be lingering by.

One other dearly held belief by Carla was that a potent memory jogger along with music would be booze. As she clomped her feet back to her apartment in the sunlight and away from The Temptations, her brain had made the full trip back in time.

Even keeled beats bounced their way toward her seat. It was a song that compelled an infectious level of foot tapping. The upside of being seated in the back corner was that Carla was out of the main attractions so she could safely roll her eyes at every one of the unnecessary five million speeches that would be delivered about the happy couple. There was one downside though, she was in the direct line of fire to the bathroom and therefore, every single guest at one point or several, depending on their age, consumption, and bladder capacity, would be inevitably making their way past her en route to relief.

Carla itched at the back of her head. She'd clipped in hair extensions tight like little soldiers standing in a row. Not for a lack of thickness, but the extensions made her unruly hair a bit more tamed and if there had ever been a reason for tame hair, it was unfortunately at large somewhere among tipsy uncles and nosy aunts. She'd considered unclipping them and abandoning them onsite. She'd thought that maybe now was her moment to escape, as the hours had dribbled by and she'd largely avoided the one, the only, Paul.

She was wrong, because as she itched away at yet another row of clip-ins, she found that there was movement to her left. And as she looked over, there he was in all his glory. A few buttons undone, an unwrapped bowtie hanging from his neck, and those infuriating dimples that framed a pearly, mischievous smile.

"And now how about seeing you here?

"Well, when your sister marries one Papas, you apparently marry them all."

"It's almost like you aren't excited to be here."

"It's almost like you're clairvoyant."

"You don't like returning to the scene of the crime?" He leaned both his elbows on the table, coming closer.

It had occurred to her that his girlfriend wasn't there, "Stop." In fact, the more she scanned the room, the clearer it was that he was presently girlfriendless. She opened her mouth, but he shortly cut her off.

"Come on, I need my drinking buddy back," he looked at her fifth nearly empty glass of prosecco. "And that ain't gonna do the trick anyway."

Carla was determined to hold strong. She was above his tricks, having been through them twice before. "I'm good," she responded coolly.

"Come on," he looked adoringly at her, "it's been ages. Like maybe we should talk."

She opened her mouth defiantly, happy to put Paul in his place. Triumphant that after all this time she would be able to do what she should have. As she continued to scan the room for the mysterious girlfriend he'd left her for repeatedly, she found her lips forming the word, "Fine." *Wait, what?*

"Great. I'll be right back."

Shit. Why did I say that? She sat back in her chair, staring at her empties, growing ever more frustrated with herself. She could stand up and walk out of the reception hall and walk herself home. Probably. She could probably walk herself home. Or Uber, whatever.

Carla sat pondering her abilities to walk home for far too long, however, because Paul had returned with three brown murky beverages and placed one in front of her. She picked it up. He had brought her a drink, so there couldn't be all that much harm in consuming it. Maybe. Probably. She sipped tenderly and decided that if she had gone through the trouble of curling her hair around extensions in a childish attempt to look good in front of her ex, that she could make him sing for his supper now that she had his attention. "So what did you need to talk about?"

His lips curled into a smile once again. "Well, you wanna go right there? I thought maybe we'd catch up for a bit."

"Okay, I paid off my student loans, I'm still working as a debt collector, Summer and Jas are married now and great. Your turn."

"Well," he clinked one of his glasses to hers. "Cheers."

They both sucked on their straws and held eye contact for a while. She could feel him looking right through her.

"I just. It feels like you're really holding something against me. It doesn't feel fair."

"Why would you care? You haven't seen me in nearly a year." *Luckily*.

"I don't get why. I'm hearing through your sister, through the grape vine that you were so pissed at me."

Nice. What a nice sister she had, running her mouth about every other thing to everyone in the immediate world. "You disappeared."

"I didn't disappear."

"You kept going off to what's-her-face." She sucked down more of the sugary confection of the drink Paul had brought her.

"How about you in all this?" He downed the remainder of the first of his glasses.

"Me? I didn't do anything." Her irritation grew at the idea she could hold any blame in any of this.

"You never texted me or called me. I felt like you weren't even interested in me."

"That's what this is all about?"

"Yeah, you didn't go out of your way at all."

"You ghosted me and then when you showed up again, I totally went with the flow."

"Well, I can't get in your head. I don't know what you're thinking."

"Obviously, I like you. Liked you." *Crap. Again.*

"So what are we doing?" He started in on the second drink and stood on his feet.

"I… Don't know." She stood up too, feeling a little wobbly. She had been aloof. That had been the answer this whole time? It had been her. The heat consumed her brain and she wobbled a bit more. He caught her by the wrists. She giggled a little at the situation. She wanted to be angry at him still for all past disappointments. But, the band had come into focus with Motown beats clunking into place, people were still laughing raucously around them, and as long as he held onto her, they were the only two people in the room. Flushed with heat, she could feel the blood pumping through her body and could hear her pulse echoing off tempo to the music in her ears.

It had been a swirl of more drinks, more jokes, and more dancing as the final hour passed and everyone made their way up to the hotel after party. And what was left there? Nobody she knew well enough to care about. Josie had returned home earlier in the night for childcare purposes and Nick remained to be seen for quite a while himself. So when the booze was nearing empty and the sun was threatening to come up, Carla found herself over the scene.

"I want to leave now."

"Where to?"

"Anywhere but this room."

"What about mine?" He stood on shaky legs.

She reached up and grabbed his hand. He pulled her up to her feet and the pair walked out like zombies.

Carla's head felt once more like a balloon, like she wasn't experiencing what was happening inside her body just as an onlooker once more. This was, of course, until she entered Paul's room, he shut the door behind them, and he once again had his hands on her. He grabbed at her face and as they kissed she unbuttoned him. Everything came off. Shirt, pants, dress, done.

They tipped over onto the bed and as his hands were incessantly running through her hair she realized something. She didn't have to live a painful life anymore, she could finally liberate her scalp of the torment of good looking hair. "One sec."

"Okay."

She sat fully up on top of him and reached a hand back; unclipping the extensions was a nearly orgasmic experience in itself. She pulled several wefts of hair out. "Oh my God, Jesus, what a relief."

"Uh, is that hair?" A very drunk Paul was looking very confused.

Aware finally of what she had done, Carla briefly came to and looked around. "Ugh, I mean… It's a whole thing… Don't worry about it." She chucked the extensions to one-side and they continued on as they had. It felt to Carla that maybe they were both right where they were meant to be.

But the feeling was fleeting. A strongly held belief that Carla came to realize in the wake of that night is that no matter how far you want to bury a feeling into your subconscious, it always comes out into the light. It will probably happen at an inconvenient moment and probably in a deeply embarrassing way.

This way would begin in the form of a knock on the door. A thump, thump, thump would be far more sobering than any cold shower. At the sound of bare knuckles thwacking into hard wood repeatedly, Carla's entire body had shot up straight as though he spine had suddenly become affixed to an iron rod.

She looked down at Paul, confused. The question that flew from her however was, "Is that your girlfriend?" *Crap. Again. Again. Again.* Embarrassing? Yes. Inconvenient? Certainly. An artifact she'd thought she had thrown away and disguised earlier in the night was not so far away after all.

"What? No."

"So that's not your girlfriend." She relaxed. Until she realized who she now was. A person who had tricked herself into thinking someone she wanted to sleep with was single, who was in actuality cheating on his girlfriend with her. *Crap. Crap. Again.*

"No," he repeated. "She's in New York."

But now, continuing on with her journey of realization, he was unfazed by this. There he was with the very person he repeatedly ghosted for the very girlfriend he was presently cheating on. "So who is that?" she nearly spat at him.

"My brother."

Carla wasn't sure why the word, *brother*, fueled her anger, but she somehow found herself fixated on it. "Your brother."

"Yeah."

"Your brother is out there?" Her voice raised and the thumping stopped.

"He is."

"And he wants to come in here."

"Yeah."

"So what you're telling me is that your brother is out there and he is gonna stay in here."

"Uh huh."

"And you have a girlfriend."

"Yes?"

Carla fell off not only Paul but the bed. "Ow, fuck!"

If repeated thumping and revelations of girlfriends and cheating hadn't been enough to sober her up, then the industrial grade carpeting of the Sonesta finished off the hat trick. So would begin her first punishment of the night from this sorry affair, a full body rug burn. She stood up and Paul sat up, looking a little worried.

"What are you doing?"

"Uh, getting dressed since I don't feel like having a little trubbie with you and your stupid brother." She pulled her dress back on and started looking for her bra.

"What's a trubbie? You always came up with the weirdest things."

She gave up on the bra and grabbed a high heel, pointing it at him and screamed at the top of her lungs. "You know what you should do, Paul? Maybe you should be single for a while. Maybe that would be good for you!" With that she grabbed her other heel and stormed out the door.

Carla had expected Paul's brother to be standing outside the door, but there was no one even there. Just a long empty hotel hallway. She ambled along, not really drunk, but not really sober.

"Carla! Wait."

Her footsteps stopped. Maybe her apology would be coming. She looked straight ahead with a mere smile playing on her lips. He would say he was sorry. Then she would. They could walk away from this mistake of a night. She made sure to clear her face of any emotion before turning around and looking at him though. "What?"

"You forgot your hair!" And there he stood, hanging out of a hotel room door in his boxers holding a fistful of hair, looking a little puzzled.

In the following days, as she suffered punishment

number two in relaying her tale to Summer and Jas, and punishment number three of vividly reliving her mistakes in her mind, she would have liked to say that she turned on her heel and stormed off.

However, the thing was, those hair extensions had run her around a hundred dollars, and while earlier in the night she had foolishly thought of abandoning them at her table with the assumption her mom might grab them, in that moment she stood in a dress from the night before, clutching her shoes, and trying to keep tears from welling up in her eyes. She wordlessly walked back to Paul, retrieved the hair extensions from him, and left without a sound.

The elevator doors closed, encasing her in a safe zone for roughly five seconds. Five seconds spent popping out fat, eyeliner stained tears. As the doors reopened, she was greeted with a baffled looking housekeeper, whom she had awkwardly dosey-doed past in order to exit. Families had arisen for that morning and a small child stared at her unabashedly as she dragged her bare feet out the door. Yet another strongly held belief came into play, this one being that one should never walk through the streets of the city barefoot. Her fourth punishment would be the toe fungus, it took a month to get rid of as she had dragged her feet through the streets of Cambridge. In too much pain physically and emotionally, Carla walked her way home in the sunlight that morning. The weather was juxtaposed against her feelings, a cruel twisted irony.

There was a thump, thump, thump pounding into Carla's door. Into her skull. She thought she'd relived that memory and it would be done. She rolled over in her bed so that her eyes would be angled away from any sunlight trying to creep around the corners of her blinds. The thumping restarted. She forced her left eye to will itself open and point at the door as though she could will away whoever was on the other side of it.

"Come on, Carla. Open up!"

Shit. It was Josie.

Carla wretched herself out of bed, tripping over her own shoes in the process of getting to the door. Anything to make the thumping stop. The locks tumbled out of place, and on her threshold a very angry Josie stood before her.

"Well, good morning, Sis."

"Wish I could say the same."

"How'd you know to come here?" Carla walked backward into her kitchen and reached for a glass, filling it with water.

"I called your office, got rerouted a couple times and eventually wound up talking to someone named Miriam."

"So you know."

"Yeah," Josie moved farther into her apartment and closed the door behind her, "I know."

"I thought one of the upsides of being unemployed was sleeping in."

"Don't be a wise ass." Josie waded through the discarded clothes on the floor and sat on the edge of Carla's bed.

Carla lumbered back into her bed and leaned against the back wall. "So why were you even looking for me at work?"

"You weren't there on Sunday."

"So? You don't show up all the time. Maybe I wanted a turn."

"Yeah, but that's the thing, Carla. I don't show up. You always do."

"I'll call Ma and say I'm sorry. Is she freaking out or something?"

"That's not the point. You're missing the point."

"You want to rub my face in something else? Is

that the point?" Carla was in no mood for anyone or anything.

"No. Don't be a brat. I'm saying- I'm asking what's wrong."

"Well, I'm unemployed, I've crashed and burned with another guy I'd been seeing, and I've let down my friends. So, basically, everything."

"That's nothing you can't fix." Josie's tone was calm, her eyes widened into huge walnuts, and she looked like she might lunge at Carla and hug her or something.

"Why are you being so nice all of a sudden?" Carla couldn't trust new Josie, who sat at the foot of her bed. Josie the mother.

"I'm not being nice *all of a sudden*."

"You always pick on me."

"No I don't!" Her faced scrunched up defensively. That was it. That was the Josie she knew.

"Yeah, you do. When we were little you never wanted to play with me, when we were teenagers you were always ditching out on all of us, and now that we're adults you're always shooing me away from all the choices I make."

"I really don't think you can hold stuff from when we were kids against me and for the record I don't shoo you away from your choices. I wanted to push you away from everything here."

"Really?"

"Yeah, really."

"That is interesting 'cause it feels like you're constantly looking down your nose at me. You and Ma."

"Ma can speak for herself. But that was never me. We didn't play when we were kids 'cause we were like oil and water. Now that we're grown up, that's really not all that different, but I don't want oil to be water. I want you to be you."

"You and Ma don't want me to be a teacher and marry a nice boy from down the street and, like, pop out a few kids and the whole deal? 'Cause I've sat through many Sunday dinners."

"Not what I want. You're oil. Go be oil. There's nothing wrong with living life at your own pace, but I gotta tell you. You're acting like a real loser right now."

"…and there it is."

"Yeah, I mean 'cause you're sitting in a dark studio apartment in the middle of a workday… smells like a brewery in here by the way."

"You've made your point."

Josie stood up. "No, I actually I don't think I have." She climbed around to the other side of the bed and yanked the blinds open.

"Oh Jesus, could you not?"

Josie kept going, "I cannot not… or whatever." She shoved the window open. "Jesus, that's better." She walked back around and snatched the glass of water from Carla's hand.

"You could get your own, you know."

"No, don't think I can." She threw the water in Carla's face.

"What the fuck!"

"Little girl, wake up. Get off your ass and stop wasting your time around here."

"God, you're so dramatic."

"You aren't doing what you want, you aren't dating who you want. If I wanted all the stuff you did, I would've been outta here years ago. You just sit around going through all the motions of some bland life that you act like you're above anyway." She walked back over to the sink and refilled the glass. She took a sip and returned to Carla's bedside.

"I'm trying!"

"No, you aren't. You're just waiting for stuff to happen to you. Waste of time." She took another sip and threw the remaining water on Carla once again.

"Okay, well, now you're just getting my bed wet."

"Good. Get out of it."

"Fine!" Carla popped up. "Happy? I'm out! Just please stop throwing water on me."

"Better. Now what are you gonna do?"

"I'll go find another job."

"Wrong. You're doing it all over again."

"Fine. What am I supposed to do? You apparently know everything."

"You're too smart and too talented to waste your life doing some sort of job behind a desk at a corporation or whatever it is you think you're gonna do. That's not what you like. Stop wasting time. Go figure it out."

"I took the job so I wouldn't be broke. Sue me."

"Don't be a dick. You know what I mean. None of this around here is even what you want. If I can see that, why can't you?"

"Because…" Carla didn't have a retort. She was tired, both in general and from her several day bender. The words flew out unencumbered, "I'm scared."

"Okay. When I was wandering around my own wedding knocked up, that wasn't not scary. But, I smiled for the cameras. You know? We all have the stuff pile up on us and we all deal."

"I don't even know where to start. I don't even have Summer to talk to."

"Well, I don't know what the deal with that is."

"I mean, I feel really bad."

"Okay, and that's the other thing."

"What?"

"You can't just keep doing crappy things and then going around saying I feel bad. You have to actually be better once in a while."

"So what does that mean?"

"If you did something to Summer, don't just go and be like 'buhhh, I feel bad.'"

"I do not even sound like that."

"You know what I mean."

Carla looked back at Josie once more. She really looked at her. Mama Josie, who she used to antagonize and spray with a hose, standing in front of her, having her back. "I guess… I guess you're right." The words just nearly killed her.

"Thank you. I know." She looked satisfied at last. Carla took a step towards her and Josie breathed in her sister. "Oh, now what're you doing?" Carla stuck both her arms out. "Oh come on, whatever you drank is, like, coming through your pores. I'm serious. It ain't pretty. And, you're all wet." But she didn't actually fight her. Josie braced herself as Carla wrapped her arms around her big sister and gave a wet, smelly hug. Yet once more, she started to let her eyes burn and tears build. Before Carla knew it, she was sobbing into her sister and her sister was holding her tight right back.

"I wish this wasn't where I was. I'm so late in the game, and I didn't even figure anything out."

Josie rocked her back and forth a little bit. "You know, Carl, there's nothing wrong with living life at your own pace."

Carla took a step back, managing to carry her weight on her own two feet. Josie ran her thumbs across the bags under Carla's eyes, wiping away the tears.

"You'll be okay. Okay?"

"Okay."

"Good," she exhaled. "Now, I gotta go pick up Joey. He and that little Ciotinelli shit set something on fire at school." With a shake of her head, she left in a most pedestrian fashion, as though the last ten minutes hadn't just happened.

Carla looked at the door her sister had left through. Josie left a ghost in her wake; the words she'd spewed out clouded above Carla's head.

She slowly did a three hundred and sixty degree turn, taking in her apartment, trying to wear Josie's eyes in doing so. A pile up of bowls and glasses sat in her sink.

Several empty liquor and wine bottles adorned the counter, there were clothes all over her floor, and her guitar was sitting on her chair. Her bathroom reeked. Her bed was a mess. Everything was a mess. So that was the impasse that she had arrived at.

Opening her solitary closet, she dragged out her hamper and started piling every piece of clothing on the floor into it. She threw the bottles into a plastic bag and ran the faucet until it was burning hot. Slowly, her apartment was restoring itself to a normal, livable state. She opened her windows as wide as possible, letting the space air out until she was content with it again. Everything still seemed too bright. She lay back down on her bed, shielding the light from her eyes. Josie was still occupying space in her mind, repeating to her that she couldn't just keep doing bad things and saying sorry. She had to actually be better.

She did need to be better. She needed to turn it around. Let the past go. Move forward and make amends. She needed her phone.

Carla reached around until her hand found it. Forcing her body into a seated position, she started in on step one. Her fingers found the Phone App and the Phonebook within it. She had exploded at Nico much like she had exploded at Paul. What did Paul do? Waited a while, bided his time, and then reached back out. They fell back into old choreography, retracing their steps as they had before.

Her own vodka infused screams echoed off the interior of her skull and she scrolled down to Nico's name. She had behaved abysmally, but now was the time to do what Josie had said and be better. Yelling at someone and hoping they didn't call back wasn't enough. What if he did call her back? Why give him the option? 'Block this Caller' sat at the bottom of his Profile card. She said goodbye and clicked it. She opened her Facebook and blocked him. Instagram? Blocked. Any social profile she could think of that he might have would be wiped from her existence. He may not know that she was rejecting him, but she did and to her surprise, it felt like enough.

There was one more task at hand. She navigated to her messages and looked at Tim's name. Part of being better must mean trying harder. Tim wasn't her first choice. He wasn't mysterious like Nico and had no swagger the way Paul did. But, he was kind, they had fun goofing around at work, and really, what was so wrong with that?

So I didn't finish that ballad I promised you, but wanna go out anyway?

Rip-off :P

It's been a packed couple of days

So I hear. Tell me about it tomorrow?

Totally, where do you want to go?

Send me your address and I'll swing by, we can go from there.

Carla sent the address and dropped her phone back onto her bed, unsure what she was doing. She felt uncomfortable, but she had been in a safe zone for quite a while and look where she was now.

Carla stared at herself in the mirror and pondered her outfit. It wasn't anything fancy, just a swishy short skirt with a top tucked casually into the front of it. She wasn't comfortable though and she was second guessing why she even cared. Tim usually saw her dressed in a full polyester ensemble; anything would look better in comparison to that.

She kept the top and switched into jeans. She needed to try just being herself and looking like herself. Her well-worn denim was herself. She felt physically comfortable once again. She walked away from her mirror and sat down on her bed, picking up her guitar and mindlessly strumming away at random chords that had no business being in the order she was placing them. Tim would be arriving any minute, but she didn't care. He wasn't even vaguely close to being at the forefront of her mind. With each strum came a memory of Summer and the planes, Jas asking her to please come to a rehearsal, and both of them looking angry and disappointed when she hadn't been there for yet another time.

A knock on the door let her know that it was time to stop strumming and start her date. A date she had been trying to convince herself to be excited about. She laid down her guitar and opened the door, finding herself greeted with a bouquet of flowers that were being held by Tim. He smiled at her and out of politeness, she smiled back.

"Hey, thanks!" She accepted the bouquet and stood back for him to walk into her apartment. "Uh here, I'll throw them in…" She looked around cluelessly "…something."

"Good to see you again."

"Totally, well, I guess you'll be seeing less of me now." No sooner had the words left her mouth then she started second guessing them. "I don't mean because, I don't want to see. I just meant because of work. Well, it isn't work any more." Shut up, shut up, shut up. Why did she care about that though? Maybe she cared more than she gave herself credit for.

"I got you." He looked around her place. "So this is Carla's place?"

"Yeah," she finally gave up trying to think of anything and grabbed a glass. "Try not to get lost."

"So would that be what you wrote my song on?"

She set the glass of flowers on her square space of counter, praying they wouldn't tip over, and glanced at the guitar on her bed. "Yeah, it's being mastered as we speak."

He just looked at her and then to the flower filled water glass.

"You wanna go?" She spoke only to break the now stilted silence.

"Yeah, let's."

The two set off. She locked her door, she jumped over the broken step, and she let Tim lead the way. He felt different now than when they were at work. Quieter, more chilled out. He wasn't joking all that much as he once did. Or speaking at all for that matter. "So where we headed? There are some spots in Porter I know of."

"I figured we'd head to Harvard."

"Nice, do you hang out there a lot?"

"Not a ton, but I know some places."

"Cool."

"So you doing anything this weekend?" They walked through late afternoon dusk and she appreciated the silence, save the sounds of the city. It was strange to be out with someone, period, as she and Nico had spent most of their time indoors.

"Well, I'll probably head down to the South Shore. My family's there in Marshfield and I'd planned on hitting the beach. You?"

"Beach sounds nice."

"Oh yeah, we have a Boston Whaler we take out and kayaks and stuff, wicked fun."

"Sounds good." They continued on their way to Harvard Square. "I don't really have plans actually," she heard herself say, "I'm basically on an indefinite weekend as we speak."

"Oh yeah, I heard that. What happened there?"

"Well, see, the thing is…" What was the thing? She could lie and say she'd been laid off. "The thing is I haven't wanted to work there for a while," she wasn't going to twist the truth into a pretzel-shaped distortion. And, she figured that would have been just what old Carla would have done. "I let everything slide. If you don't bring in money, they don't need you, and so now, I don't work there any more."

He bobbed his head up and down, nodding. "Well, okay," he laughed.

Why hadn't she just said that before? Or something to that effect to everyone about everything? What had she been afraid of? Tim screaming and running away like a madman? "Yeah, it's been time for a while."

"What're you gonna do now, though?"

She smiled, looking at him again, "You know what? I'm not totally sure."

"That's not, like, scary to you or anything?"

"It's not comfortable."

"Yeah, I'll say. I dunno what I'd do in that situation."

They arrived closer to their final destination. She could see bricks arranged into the ground up ahead. "Coincidentally, I don't know what I'm doing." Her steps felt bolder as she made the admittance a second time.

"I guess I just like having my safety net, you know?"

"I hear you, man, I always did too." Another couple minutes passed and they had reached the heart of the Square. Buses careened down curved old roads while students and tourists darted from one side of the street to the other in a high-stakes game of frogger. The sun was starting to make its break for it and run on over to California. Wrought iron street lamps illuminated themselves on command. It would've been a beautiful night, with light dancing all around and the soundtrack of the city pumping noise around their heads and blood through her heart. She looked up at Tim, wanting to want him. He hadn't even bolted when she confirmed she was jobless. He made jokes about music instead of taking it too seriously. She could talk about anything on her mind.

"So, where do you wanna go?" She looked around, kind of curious, as these weren't her normal parts. "There a place called Beat Brew Hall around the corner here. They have good live music some nights. Or maybe it's every night." She looked around. "Well, it's around there, I think. This place is such a maze if you don't come here often."

"You don't come here often?"

"Naw, I usually hang by Porter."

"Oh," he looked confused. "I didn't think there was even anything to do there, but, you know, I'm in Brighton."

"Yeah, that's a hike."

"Yeah, it's cool though. I was thinking we'd go to Fire and Ice."

"Oh. You mean the place where you pick raw food and they stir fry it on a big grill in front of you?"

"Yeah! I love that place."

"I thought it was in the Back Bay?"

"Well, there's one here too." He beckoned her to one side, and she followed. "I come here almost every time I'm around this area."

"Really?"

"Totally."

Fifteen minutes later, there they stood in a line with their thirty closest friends as sweat-laden chefs arranged everyone's bowls of food into neat little soldier-like lines on an enormous circular grill. She had to give it to them, she wouldn't have wanted to stand next to a hot grill sautéing various configurations of the same foods and sauces for an entire shift. She wondered how much they hated the sight of diced meats, veggies, and pastas. And the stench. They'd been there for not even an hour, but Carla was certain she would walk out reeking like a combo of parmesan cream, curry, and pepper sauces.

They sat down; her mind was mostly consumed by an impending shower. But she ate and chatted and learned that Tim had, in addition to a love of aquatic sport, a penchant for following local Boston teams, assumed that in a few years he'd a own a home, hopefully near where he grew up, and eventually wanted kids; if they didn't love hockey as much as he did he would be *bummed.*

Of course, that's when the conversation returned to her. "What's your family like?"

"Well, my dad used to work in construction and my mom worked in the office of an elementary school. I mean neither of them do that anymore. They're both retired. Now mostly my Mom cooks, asks me when I'm gonna get married, and tries to talk me into going back to school to be a teacher."

"Teaching wouldn't be so bad, right? I mean they get pensions and summers."

"Yeah, I just never saw myself doing that."

"Well, if you're in between jobs, that could be a thing you could do."

"I'm just not sure, like, going to work every day, and heading straight home to do the dinner-by-six-thing every night sounds like it's for me."

"No?" He looked bewildered. "But eventually, maybe?"

She shook her head no and tried to take a huge bite full of her meal to make it go away faster. Tim had managed to swallow his whole plate by this point.

"What do you think you'll do then?"

He seemed to be really fixated on that. The answer was the same though. She shrugged once again and marveled at how gently the words tumbled out of her, "I don't know."

"What did you want to do before?"

"I studied music for the year that I went to school."

"What were you planning on doing after that?"

"Well, I, you know, I wasn't sure, so I stopped because I needed to work and make money and everything. But, that's still where my heart is."

"Cool, so you mean that's why you were always doodling?"

"Yeah, actually," her voice dropped an octave as

she thought about Summer. "My friend Jas and I were gonna enter a competition."

"That's cool."

"Yeah, I haven't managed to- well it's been hard to write." That lie managed to still slip out. She had written more than enough. She failed to show up. That was the problem.

"'Cause of work stuff?"

"Yeah," lie number two for the night.

"I'm sure you could always just catch back up with him. Can't he just write the song and you perform it?"

"I'm a songwriter." Not a lie. "That's what I want to be." She hated saying it out loud. All other truths had felt good that night. Admitting what she wanted didn't.

"Then… I'm sure you'll figure it out." He slid to the side of his booth. "I'm gonna grab another plate. You wanna join?"

"No, thank you. I got really full."

"Alright," he shrugged.

She sat there and looked down at her phone, remembering Jas and his bandmates, all the times he'd called her to go and rehearse, and all the times she'd let him down. Josie's words returned for yet another round of 'make Carla feel guilty.' Be better. Josie was right, it was annoying, and it was also amazing the qualities from their mother she managed to inherit and emulate so accurately.

Her night was only half over with Tim; he eventually returned and she watched him happily plow through another plate of food. She laughed at his jokes, because as he had pretended to understand that she wanted to pursue music, she pretended to be interested in the tales he had from the annual family cruises he would go on. They grabbed fro-yo after dinner at his behest and they covered everything from movies, buddy comedies being his favorite, to preferred bars, she cited Thursday night jazz at Wally's. They even made it to every MBTA commuters' paramount indulgence of complaining about the T.

Eventually, it was time to go home, and Tim, being the gentleman that he was walked her back to her door. And there they were at the end of an appropriate, traditional, respectful date. She looked up at him and he leaned down and kissed her. It was… serviceable.

She hated that she thought that. He pulled back afterward and smiled down at her, pleased. "Thanks for a fun night."

"No," Carla said, "thank you."

"Goodnight." He took a step back. "I'll see you again."

She knew she would be a jerk and even more so, a fool, to say now, "Yes. Of course." She stepped back toward her stairs and watched him walk back down the street. One more pace back and she landed in the broken step. "Fuck."

SHAKE IT OUT

"I guess the thing is that I spent all the time with this guy. We were on and then off." Carla could've stopped there probably, but she thought better of it. She was in a weird mood. A sharing mood. "And then we were on again and off again… Until we were on for that one last explosive time. And since then we've been off forever. Turns out, when you drunkenly rip the weave out of your hair and then have sex with someone and then scream at him and *then* run away after retrieving your weave, he doesn't really have any interest in seeing you again after that. But, you know, I've been doing, like, *a lot* of thinking lately, so I saw what I was doing. I saw where I was headed. Oh, sorry, to answer your question, I'd been dating this new guy. Yeah, the new guy though, he wasn't really so great. Kinda could've fit into the mold of any self-important loser who walked off the street. I didn't realize it at the time. Sometimes it's hard to realize stuff as it's happening, you know? Anyway though, I blocked him. I gotta say, it was wicked liberating. I didn't tell him to go to hell, which would have been ideal, but at the least I got to have the last word. Which is technically no word, but essentially it's still a last word." Her mind wandered to her date last week. "But then there was this other guy, Tim. He's really sweet. We went on a date to this place called Fire and Ice. It's awful, but he actually planned something and he paid. That part was kinda weird. I could've done with splitting. I know I'm unemployed and everything now, but I can still pay for things. I felt," she paused. How had she felt? "I felt guilty. You know? Like all these people I grew up with, they all got married and had kids and stuff and then there's Tim. Sitting across from me while we eat overcooked institutionalized food drenched in lardy alfredo sauce telling me he wants all those things and all I wanted to do was, like, get out of there as fast as possible. I don't get how everyone else I know could be already settled in their lives, knowing exactly what to do. But I'm either ripping my weave out of my hair, dating morons, or rejecting nice guys. I think there's something wrong with me. OUCH!"

Carla looked down at her feet in stirrups, a paper apron over her legs. Glenda's head popped up and she passed off a clear tube containing a bit of Carla's cervix in it to a nurse. A nurse who looked as though she was working overtime trying to suppress an eye roll. Dr. Glenda picked up a clipboard. "Well Carla, you've been coming here for the last ten years. If it makes you feel any better, we all got married young too. Then we all got divorced."

"Oh, I'm sorry?"

"That's not what I mean. You should probably just trust your instincts more than you are. If you aren't living that life, there's a reason for it."

"Never really thought of it like that."

"Well, getting back to my original question, you're saying you've had three partners since I saw you last? The answer is three?"

"Oh! No, I didn't sleep with all those people

recently. Well, one of them I did and the other one I did but not in the last year and then the third one, the nice guy I'm supposed to want to marry-"

"-I already gave you my thoughts on that-"

"-never hooked up with him."

"Okay, well the pap smear reveals all anyway."

Carla plunked back down into her reclined position. "Something to look forward to."

"If anything comes up, we'll give you a call. Do you have any other questions for me?"

"When does this all get better?"

And with that Dr. Glenda erupted into a fit of laughter and walked out the room, merely offering, "I'll see you in a year."

Carla left the doctor's office with a twenty-dollar copay, a vow to visit every doctor she could before her insurance expired, and another thought to sink her teeth into. Dr. Glenda had piled onto her sister's words, supporting the thought that she needn't feel bad for not wanting someone she felt she was supposed to want. She could go forth with Tim and carry on, get a new job, get married, acquire a mortgage and maybe make some babies, but that would be safe. Carla could be comfortable; she'd been comfortable for quite a while and it hadn't been going particularly well for quite some time. Being uncomfortable could be just what the doctor ordered. There were two people who hadn't shared their opinions with her on the topic. It was her fault and she knew she needed to be better. Plus, she missed Summer and Jas.

Carla donned a sundress, grabbed an oversized, ripped denim jacket and laced up her chucks. She plugged buds into her ears, chose Foo Fighters' "Walking After You" and let the quiet steady drumbeats climb their way through the wires and up to her ears. The quiet whisper-grumble of a male voice joined in after a few moments and Carla gave herself one more nervous look in the mirror before setting off to the red line. She didn't know why she'd even bothered looking at her appearance, she was off to pay penance to Jas. As though Jas cared about what anything looked like.

It was the middle of the day on a Tuesday, so the streets in her neighborhood were devoid of people as was the red line when she boarded the train. She attempted to focus on only her music so as not to fret about the impending conversation. It was hard though; to not let her mind wander about. Confrontation had once been natural for her. It was why once upon a time she had been such an effective debt collector. Time had worn that away and she was well out of practice. On a normal day she would've been beyond annoyed to have to make the trek all the way to Fenway, but now she savored every moment of her impending apology.

The green line, the bane of every commuter's existence. It screeched its way down the grubby, dank tunnels and groaned as it went around corners. A little boy in a Red Sox hat held his ears as his eyebrows scrunched in pain. *You look how I feel, Buddy.* The car came to a final grinding halt, completing the move only with one final resounding screech.

Carla stood up and lumbered down the steps and out of the train. It was sweltering on the platform; the humid tunnel air consumed and suffocated her. She exited via the escalator and found herself emerging into a dry burning sun. She dragged her feet, each step landing hard onto the pavement. Over the bridge that loomed above the Mass Pike, she ripped out the earbuds and stood for a moment. The music seemed to be only noises that clanged in her head, mixing with her thoughts, and making no sense. It was a jumbled mess that left her mind cluttered. There was a slight breeze though that also could have just been the exhaust fumes from the highway. The mixing of words and melodies finally stopped as she took deep breathes and focused on the roaring traffic that whooshed below.

She proceeded forward to Guitar Center. It was empty at the moment due to the time of day, a purposeful choice that Carla had made. She walked past the electric guitars. New and old, they beamed at her. Percussion was off to one side and she saw a kid going ham on a drum kit, though the sound could reach her. Looking around the counter, she saw no Jas. It wasn't until her complete one-eighty that she saw Jas properly. He was loading guitar straps onto a display off to the side.

She could have sworn she was taking steps forward, but it could've been the earth moving below her. "Hey?"

"Can I help y-" He stopped as realization passed over his eyes. "Oh, hey."

"Hey Jas."

"You're a long way from home."

"Well, I needed to talk to you."

"I'm working right now."

"I know, but I figured if I came now, then it wouldn't be busy and you'd hear me out."

"So you came when it was slow enough to talk to me."

"Yeah."

"And why'd you come to my work? So I was trapped here, having to speak with you?"

"No." *Yes.*

"What do you want?"

"I'm… sorry."

"Okay. Great." He turned away and started walking.

Carla followed him as he reached the counter. "I'm serious, Jas. I know I've been acting like a dick."

"Heard that before."

"I know I ditched you and your band and I said

I'd come when you needed me to."

"Yeah, you did do that. We were depending on you, and you more or less told us to fuck off. And, by the way, no one *needed* you. This would have been good for you. I stuck my neck out for you. And Summer." He stopped getting riled up. It was state she'd rarely seen him in, a reason why she'd been dreading this all along.

"I can't even explain why I've been hiding from Summer. But you gotta know the reason I didn't come was 'cause I never found the words."

"You were off chasing that Nico douche. Don't play me like that."

"Yeah, and no. I couldn't find the words that I needed though. I haven't been able to write. I haven't been able to do anything for ages."

"You have an awful lot of excuses for why you didn't do something very simple."

"I know. I know. I didn't show up."

"It isn't just this you didn't show for, Carla. You haven't shown up for a long ass time."

"I haven't, I know."

"I don't think you do. I don't think you get why Summer was so upset with you. You haven't shown up for life in a while. This was something you could have been a part of. We could have built something together."

She looked at Jas' frustrated face. That was just it though, where she'd expected to see anger she was surprised to find only frustration. "I know I've just been existing for a while now."

"So are you planning on doing anything about it? That why you're here?"

"Yes!" She threw up her hands, "Jesus."

"Oh really? That's a magical overnight change. Gonna stop dating morons, move into an apartment that isn't also a death trap? Gonna quit your job."

"I got fired, so I guess they did it for me. Okay? Happy?"

Jas sighed, "No."

"Well, I'm shocked, it seems like you'd think I deserve that."

"No."

"Whatever. I just came to say I *am* sorry. I know I owe Summer a bigger apology." She'd at least had an inkling of how to do that. Jas was turning out to be the bigger puzzle. "I'm gonna go now." She made toward the doors.

"I wanted you to quit."

She turned and looked at him.

"I want you to show up to practice and find a job you like and date someone worthwhile. So does Summer."

"Thanks."

He crossed his arms. "It's…. It's fine. Carla, it's fine."

"Okay, thanks." She continued to walk to the doors and then thought better of it and looked back again. "If I found my words, could I swing by maybe? Like one day?"

"Don't leave me hanging."

"I won't."

"Again."

"I promise." She silently swore it up and down and she walked out the door.

Her trip back to the T would bring her over the bridge; she paused again. Be better, don't date idiots, live in a grown up apartment. The job was gone, so that step was taken care of. She looked down at the cars flying underneath the bridge; she leaned into the wire that held her back. In a few hours, that road would be gridlocked, filled with half-asleep commuters who spent an hour to travel fifteen minutes out from their jobs to their grown up apartments. She knew she wasn't allowed to pass judgment because she'd barely been any different.

Carla also knew that a change was in the future. She looped her fingers into the caging and pressed her forehead against the wire. How many more years would she go on like she had, but at a different company and with worse hours and a farther distance to travel? What was the point? A change was certainly coming, but she decided in that moment that she wouldn't allow one more thing to *happen* to her. If she stayed here, everything would only ever happen to her. She could fall on her face again, but at least it would be her choice, too. She pushed herself back from the barrier and took her phone out. She had a call to make.

She waited through the beeps, but was greeted only by voicemail. Carla took a deep breath, "Hey, I was wondering if I could come stay with you for a little bit. I'm in between jobs and just trying to figure some stuff out. Not for long, I swear. Just until I can get myself settled. Let me know what you think. And uh, just please don't mention this to Summer until I can talk to her? Thanks."

Sunday dinner had arrived and Carla marched in through the front door. Her nose was greeted by the familiar smells of garlic and the citrus of tomato. Her ears met the usual cacophony of clanging pots and pans, a local news station, and today the tunes of Sting. She slid out of her shoes at the door and felt the floorboards on the bottom of her feet, taking note of every moment and making a memory of everything she could.

Carla had had quite a few sleepless nights. It was hard to be sleepless when you didn't have a television, as there's very little left to fill those waking hours. So she doodled a lot, slowly stringing her words together more and more, keeping the lines rather than crumpling each one and sending it to the trash. But the high-spirited D and G that rang out from her guitar in the early hours of the morning were airy and happy, light and glowing. They were the sunset in her photo of a Los Angeles beach. The color melted from the picture and poured into her eyes; it flew from her finger tips and they played against the guitar. She had many things still on her mind. Jas had wanted her to quit; Josie wanted her to be better. There was one big opinion she hadn't heard from- Summer. It was still too scary to her go and speak with her.

"Ma?"

"Oh? Is that Carla?" She heard the voice cut through the noise and come bounding back down the hall at her.

"Yeah, it's me."

"Oh, goodness. Look at you." Her mom pulled her into a tight hug. Carla lay a cheek into her mom's shoulder and breathed in the garlic that had woven itself into the fabric of her shirt. Her mother didn't just hug, she enveloped you and let you forget the whole world existed. You could be a kid again. It was mom magic. "You must've been down for the count there, huh?"

"What?"

"Well, Josie told us how sick you'd gotten." Her mother loosed her embrace and released her. "Probably all that crap you eat." She turned on her heel, muttering, "You've really gotta start cooking your own food, you know."

Carla followed her mother into the kitchen and walked toward the sauce pot, but found it empty. "Where's the-"

"Table."

Whirling around on her heel, she found Josie reclining on a chair, gravy and meatballs sitting in a large bowl in front of her. Joey and Antonietta ran back and forth outside, yelping about.

"You beat me."

"I figured it was my turn. How're you feeling, sicko?"

"Fine. I'm all good now."

Ana marched a salad bowl over to the table.

"Well, now isn't this nice? Having both my girls home at once, finally. It's been forever." She looked up at the ceiling and screamed, "Joe!" They all waited a minute, but heard no thumping to speak of. "God, that man is deaf as a haddock." The stout woman marched back and continued to scream her husband's name.

"I was sick for two weeks?" Carla smirked at Josie

"Yeah, must've been, like, E.coli or something."

"I owe you a thank you."

"You do?"

"Yeah, I realized a lot of things. I thought about what you said and everything."

Josie clutched her chest in faux shock, "You *listened* to me? Oh my God. I think hell's frozen over."

"I couldn't get it all out of my head. And then, ugh, I was on this awful date with the nicest guy, but like, I mean the date was not right-"

"What's this?" Her mother had returned with her father in tow. "Did you say, *date?*"

"What date?" her father piped in.

"Carla went on a date. I just heard it. How'd it go?"

"He was fine. It was nice."

"Well, that's good!"

"Nice is not good. No one wants to be called nice," Josie piped in.

"Josephine, do not discourage your sister from dating," she barked out before softening her tone and addressing Carla once again. "So where's he from?"

Carla sighed, not wanting to get into any of this, "The South Shore."

Her father sat down as Josie went outside to gather her kids. "The South Shore?"

"Yeah."

"Oh… Well, I guess no one's perfect."

"Oh stop," her mother was sitting next to her, shooting laser beams of encouragement out of her eyes.

"And what does he do?"

"He's in accounting, but it wasn't good. Like at all."

"Well, why not?"

"It's just, a whole lot of things."

Saved by the Joey. The little guy flew in the house, giggling maniacally as Josie and a mud-slung Antonietta lumbered in after him, the latter looking slightly less pleased.

"Look at you!" she exclaimed.

"I got her!"

"Ugh," grumbled Antonietta. "I give up." Covered in mud, she sat at the dinner table.

"Well, I'm glad one of you is taking after your Auntie."

"I'm starving."

"I'm also starving."

With that, everyone found the appropriate chairs, genuflected where appropriate, and dug in. Her mother hesitated, clearly wanting to segue back into their initial conversation. "So no new man?"

"Nope. No new man. Just a disappointing date."

"Well, that's too bad," she looked disappointed. "Anything else going on besides the stomach issues?"

"I'm no collector," she heard herself say.

"You're not?" her father asked.

"Oh, did you think about teaching again?"

The next few words erupted from her before she could stop them, "And I'm moving to California."

Time could have possibly stopped. Her heartbeat jumped into her ears and her mother's mouth fell open. Her father stopped eating and stared at her, confused, while Josie dropped her fork and slowly started to smile.

"California. That's all the way on the other side of the country."

"Yep," Carla was relieved someone had said something. Even if it was Antonietta.

"How come?"

The million-dollar question goes to the kid. "Well, sometimes, you can get stuck in a rut and you need something new and some new people around you to shake it all up again."

"Why would you need new people?" her mother bellowed out at her. "Why would you want to leave me? Are we not enough for you?"

"No, Ma," Carla winced.

"And why does something new have to mean being practically on the other side of the world?" her father demanded.

"Do you know how much plane tickets cost, Carla?"

"What? Yeah, of course."

"How will you get home?"

"Where are you going to stay?

"You'll need a car."

"I just don't see why this is necessary."

"It's all that reality TV you watch, Ana. And the cell phone. Those can't be good for you."

"I suppose you're gonna shoot up your face with Botox next."

"I heard they'll give you cancer."

"The implants too, you'll be doing that soon enough."

"I gotta say," Josie interrupted, "this isn't the worst idea she's ever had."

"Oh, stop it Josephine, you don't know what you're talking about."

"Ma, relax. I'm not disappearing forever. Just for a while."

Her mother stood up. "But, well." She looked like her eyes may have filled with tears. They widened and her lips were firmly pressed together. "What's gonna happen around Christmas?" She sniffed.

Carla stood up too so she was eye level with her

mom. "I'm gonna come back for Christmas. I promise. Look. I need a change, a big one. Things aren't going well for me here. Nothing in fact. Not for jobs, not for dating, nothing. I'm gonna crash with Arlo. He said I could until I get on my feet."

"But what will you do there?"

"What am I doing here?"

Carla smoothed the covers over her bed. She pulled her chair away from it and moved her guitar and stand off to the side as well. She held up her phone and took a photo of the perfectly made bed. Looking at the result, she felt dissatisfied. Nothing really looked as good when it was photographed at night. Then she realized she was taking photos for Craigslist, so it really didn't matter.

The time had worn on that afternoon. Her parents had more questions, all of which she answered, though each time it was dissatisfying to her. Josie stood up and said her piece for Carla, continuing on her streak of thoroughly confusing behavior. Antonietta and Joey seemed at least to come out of the night with a win as they were able to eat as much ice cream as they wanted so long as the grown ups were busy standing around yelling at each other.

Eventually, everyone's voice wore out, the kids were getting tired and Carla's parents came to understand that arguing would be futile. She hugged them goodbye, and though her mother's body was a little bit stiffer initially after forcibly hugging her for a moment longer, her muscles relaxed and she gave Carla a little rock back and forth before saying goodbye.

What was left was for her was to separate and package her belongings, sell off what she could, and give the rest away. Posting it was premature at this point. Her plane ticket was for three weeks from now. It was the end of the summer and she would start new in a different city in autumn, the day after the song contest.

Jas had told her she could still come back and play with them. She needed to find her words though. She opened her one cabinet and took out the few plates and bowls she had, leaving only one of each type of plate and utensil. The rest went in boxes and would be handed over to Josie. She had certainly written more than enough, but nothing was strung together, and finding a way to end it all was the hardest part.

She looked at the wall that was covered in her photos. Those, after her guitar and some clothes, would be joining her on her trip out west. The pictures of her and Summer as kids, her squirting Josie with the hose, and family holidays spent together year after year. She took each one down, trying her hardest to relive the memory contained in it. Eventually, her shoebox was chock full of snippets from her life. One picture remained, the image she had once captured on a California beach. She left it there to hang and reclined on her bed, looking at it until she could finally bring herself to fall asleep.

Carla knew she couldn't just go to Summer and Jas empty handed. She needed an offering for them, something to prove her penance. She sat down on her mattress, which was now on the floor, and plucked once more at her guitar strings. She flopped open her notebook and scribbled a little bit; there wasn't much to the ramblings though.

I got fired from my job
It sucks sure, I've got a prob-lem
I'm swaying more on a stormy sea

Soon I'll be short on cash
My head is stressed but my heart is brash

This boat is tipping more, it might lose me

She wasn't sure if that was a good look, but she figured she'd start with something real that had happened and go from there. Time wore on. Of course, she was unemployed, and though she'd hated her job and couldn't't' have cared less to never set foot in the varying shades of grey that populated her cubicle again, she'd come to learn that it occupied a great deal of time in her life and a great deal of her life.

Tim, being the perfect guy, followed up with a text message the very next day. Initially putting in the effort to respond, her time standing on the overpass had come and gone and she resolved the matter simply by telling him she was moving to California. It had become her favorite thing to say to people. It was a magical reason that seemed to excuse her from nearly every commitment anyone wanted from her. She stood taller and had no problem being friendly to any one person who approached her in a bar. It was so easy to be charming with someone when you knew your time with them would be short-lived at best.

And as she thought of this and dared to write more words down on the page, there was of course, one person who she hadn't pronounced this happy fact to. This was made all the more worse that her plans involved staying with this person's very brother. She didn't know why she was so afraid of apologizing to her and saying goodbye. Summer was her best friend, a partner in crime, a sister. Those were all the reasons she should have felt right at home with telling her everything in her life, but they were also the reasons she dreaded it the most. She'd never seen her best friend so properly disappointed in her, and they'd never gone so long without speaking. It was a striking fact when taking into account their advanced ages and length of friendship.

That would have to be the ending of the song

right there. She dropped her pen on top of the notepad. She would need to marinate it for just one night, but there was something else she could do now. Something for Summer. She opened the lid on her laptop and found her way to Google. Writing out a feeling could get easily stuck and lodged in a lump. It took a level of detachment from the work to be able to produce something with ease and this would be her peace offering. She would make her amends and she refused to arrive empty handed.

Several days later, Carla marched through the door of a bedraggled, underused bookstore, holding her guitar and a bag. Two tables had been hastily set up and a sign that had been emblazoned with the words, "coffee" and "muffins" hung in the window. She walked past bookshelves that were still collecting dust, and was beyond shocked to see someone standing opposite Summer before her. A customer. He thanked her and picked up the bag, which she could only assumed contained a muffin, and gave the half-hearted "I'm friendly" grimace to Carla as he passed her on his way out the door.

"So, do you think he'll figure out that's just from BJ's?"

Summer looked up from that cash register with raised eyebrows that immediately fell upon realizing the voice she heard belonged to Carla. "That's what you're starting with?"

For what felt like the millionth time, Carla opened her mouth and said two simple words, "I'm sorry."

"Seen that movie. Spoiler alert, I know how this ends."

"No. Don't be like that, please." Carla walked forward to meet her at the counter.

"I can be however I want to be. I've been watching you spin around for long enough. I've reached out to you and you just do the same shit over and over, again and again. I'm tired. We're all tired."

"I know, I apologized to Jas."

"Yeah, I know. Glad you could squeak me in last."

"You aren't last."

"Yeah," her voice grew more intense, "I really am. I know you called Arlo."

"You know? Well, I wish he hadn't told you! I wanted to. I asked him not too."

"Well, Carla he's *my* brother and it's been a couple weeks now. I mean, I know I balled you out and we haven't really spoken since then, but I thought you'd at least drop me a line if you were gonna, you know, move across the country and crash at my brother's place."

"I didn't tell you right away because I don't care or anything. Actually, it's the opposite. It's a scary thing to do something new and different and shake up the scene."

Summer held out her arms, "Well no shit, glad you could join us all."

"But I'm trying to be better now. We've never had a fight like this."

"You've never been so flaky before. I mean seriously, it's always been hard to watch you through life going up and down and everything, but lately, really? I can't with that."

"Let me say it again, I know I've been a flake and I'm sorry. And I know the day with the planes should've been the game changer. I know that was the day. But I worked through it all in my head. I know what I've been doing wrong. I was afraid to tell you the most. I just felt like I lost my best friend and I wanted to figure out a way to make it up to you before I just started wandering back to you and Jas… Again."

Summer and Carla locked eyes for a minute before the chainmail dropped and Summer leaned forward, slumping onto the counter, into her familiar pose of chin-over-hands-over-elbows. "So," her head bobbed up and down. "Got any master plans before the big move date?"

"Actually yes."

"Cool, so does that mean you're gonna be like my personal wench for another two weeks?"

"No."

"It was worth a shot," she shrugged and the two, finally, broke into a mild laugh.

"I have something for you though," Carla dug into her bag. "I know you didn't know how or where to start. Not that I'm a whole genius or that this is perfect or whatever, but here." She plopped a stapled stack of paper under Summer's nose.

Summer straightened up and opened the packet, looking over it. "It's a business plan?"

"I tried to make it. It's got some empty spots, not gonna lie. But most of it is done, you just have to fill in the blanks with your personal stuff."

"Well, thank you."

"Sure."

Summer kept looking through the packet, "Carla, I'm sorry I iced you out."

"I'm sorry I acted like a dick."

"You're not a dick. I shouldn't've called you out like one."

"Yeah, you should have." Carla hoisted up her guitar bag. "If everyone let me get away with everything, I'd probably be sitting in the same crappy studio, looking for some other bland job, and dating jackasses."

"That is true. You know, like now you can whittle away all your savings until you're homeless on the beach somewhere."

"Exactly. See? I'm glad you're on board."

"So were you planning on serenading me or something?" Summer eyed the guitar.

"Jas actually. It's about time I actually showed up to a practice, you know, before we play at the song contest."

"So just in time to leave, you decide to follow through. You're breaking our hearts."

"Purple Salmon later? Or tomorrow?"

"I 'spose I need to cram all the Carla I can in now, huh?"

"You bet." She smiled, turned and made her way to where Jas practiced. She had a song she needed to sing.

ITCHIN' ON A PHOTOGRAPH

"You've been awfully quiet today." Carla's dad looked over at her.

"I dunno." She pulled both her knees into chest, the seat belt dug into her lap. "I'm kinda nervous."

"About what?"

"The fifth grade talent show."

"Oh come on! You know all those other kids are a bunch of talentless hacks."

This made Carla smile just a little bit. They were on their way back from another trip to watch the planes land, weaving their way up the streets through Orient Heights.

"Cheer up! Wanna go to iHop?"

"Like a secret iHop trip?" Her eyes lit up.

"Yeah, a super-secret iHop trip."

"Okay!"

Up Route One they went, the quick paced rumbling of Cs and Gs and A minors came on as her dad turned up the volume on The River and they started Eagle Eye Cherry's "Save Tonight." Carla wasn't totally sure what was going on in the song; she couldn't even understand half of what the singer was saying, but she liked the monotone drone of the chorus as he seemingly harmonized with himself. The high-pitched whine of a guitar solo entered into the picture at the tail of the song, when they were about to pull off the highway.

"I like that part." Carla announced as they left the off ramp onto side streets and Pearl Jam started to demand to know where oh where their baby went.

"What part?"

"The part at the end where the guitar goes wheeeee oooooh wheeee ohhhhh." She did her best impersonation.

"The guitar solo? You like guitar solos?"

"I guess I do."

"I have a nice stack of old records you should dig through then."

"Like CDs?"

"Like enormous black CDs. They're made of something called vinyl."

"Cool."

Her dad laughed and pulled into the parking lot that housed a blue roofed building. "Ready Fred?"

"I'm Carla."

Her dad angled out of the car. "Alright then. Come on, Carla."

She trotted after him into the restaurant; the pleasant smell of sugar and buttery goodness hit them and made her instantly happy. They were luckily placed in a booth and not a table.

"So you're afraid to sing in front of everyone?"

"Yeah, kinda."

"You sing at home all the time."

"Yeah, but that's just with you and Ma and Josie, and she doesn't even pay attention to me anyway."

"Well, maybe you just need some practice?"

"But I've been practicing."

"No, I mean real live in front of strangers practice."

"How do I do that?"

"Ain't no time like the present, Kiddo."

She blushed, "In here?"

"You probably know half the songs on the radio, 'cause your sister doesn't stop playing them. Just pick a song and sing it."

"But everyone's gonna stare at me and think I'm weird." She felt a little frightened.

"That's why we came to this iHop."

"Huh?"

"Notice we didn't go to the normal one in Revere? We're in Danvers."

"I thought that was just because that one burnt down and you said now it smells like a factory."

"The point is, no one's gonna remember you in Danvers. So, you might as well just give us all a good show."

She looked around. The restaurant was nearly empty at any rate. There was an older couple sitting in one corner and three teenagers who had most likely ditched lunch period in another. She looked up at the speaker. They had been blasting out oldies, and "Don't Look Back in Anger" had crept into the lineup.

She whisper-sang the first line of the chorus.

"Come on, you've got a set of pipes on you. I've heard them."

"I don't know."

"Yeah, you do! Close your eyes if it helps."

And that was what she did. She closed her eyes and audibly sang another line, begging some unspecified person to not throw it all away by putting their life in the hands of a rock and roll band.

"There you go, Kiddo. Try a little louder."

The bridge came and she did her best to match Noel Gallagher's level of loud. By the end of it she was standing. She still had her eyes closed, but that was just fine. With her eyes shut she could only see her mom and dad and Josie. They'd all be sitting there together and for once they wouldn't be hollering at one another. Her voice grew louder and she felt her way up to a standing position on the booth.

"Ugh, Carl?"

It was too late though; Carla was smiling as she blindly stood on top of a booth in a Danvers iHop scream-singing Oasis out to the heavens. It was most likely one of the most atrocious sounds the elderly couple or those teenagers had ever heard, but by the time Carla had pronounced the final lyrics of the song, she opened her eyes to see her father delighted and a waitress taken aback.

"Uhm, sir?"

"Good job Carla, gotta sit down now though."

She looked around, feeling pleased and crouched down on her legs.

"Time for pancakes."

She happily shoved the pancake in her mouth and she and her dad rumbled back down the highway on their way home, singing more relics of the nineties.

"You're quiet… Too quiet."

"Even these days, I still get a little nervous."

"Don't be. We practiced, you've got this."

Carla and Jas stood alongside his bandmates staring at the curtain they would eventually be walking through and performing on the other side of.

"Yeah, it's just been a while since I've done, well, you know, anything at all."

"If it makes you feel better, you wrote really basic beats and lyric construction," one of Jas' bandmates chimed in.

"Thank you?"

"Doing what I can to help," he bobbed his head in tune with the band that was currently playing.

"Thank you guys, by the way. I mean for learning everything on a last minute notice."

"Totally," said Jas, "Let's be honest, the guy in front of us is tearing through some Jimmy Hendrix level riffs, it isn't like we're beating most of these people. So, let's have fun and you can get your feet wet, you know?"

"Yeah," Carla's voice echoed, "totally."

The second coming of Jimmy wrapped up his set and the host went into whatever comedy bit he was trying to peddle between acts. Their name was announced and they dutifully marched out on stage. She wasn't sure if the lights were just really hot or if the sweat beading on her forehead was due more to an anxiety-induced high blood pressure. She approached the mic, which was currently positioned on a stand and wished in that moment that she had poor eyesight. If her vision was blurry, she could just live in a state of blissful ignorance. She had her iHop technique though. The highly inventive technique of closing your eyes. So she took a deep breath and did just that. She told herself she couldn't do it for the whole song, but there was nothing wrong with a little warm up, right?

With her eyes closed she was a kid again. Standing in her living room, she had the captive audience of her parents and sister. She didn't have to chase Josie around with a hose to get her attention and there wasn't yet a reason to monitor the sauce pot. She plucked at the strings on her guitar and opened her mouth wide.

I met him in the spring
I thought he'd show me many things
But I slowly learned that he'd just slip away

I put my pen to paper

But each word I wrote felt lamer
So my thoughts would have to wait for another day

Jas' bass kicked into action and was shortly joined by some drums and a second guitar. The music moved through her and through the room. She flipped her eyes open and was relieved to see that no one had run for the door.

A sailing ship across the sea
Where I wondered it'd take me?
I thought I'd found someone who could reflect
I looked around I was riding alone
He was an ass and I didn't know
I was heading for a life stage soundcheck

I got fired from my job
It sucks sure, I've got a prob-
Lem I'm swaying more on a stormy sea

Soon I'll be short on cash
My head is stressed but my heart is brash
This boat is tipping more, it might lose me

A foundation I'd built so strong
The deck boards break, shit I was wrong
I'm fearing choices that might get me wrecked
Money's great but I do declare
Something's missing it's just not there
I think what I might need is a life stage soundcheck

My friends reach and they buzz me
But I'm tired I hope they'll leave
The ship's gone down I just need a nap

In my home I waste the days
Nothing clicks cause I'm in a haze
After all these years I've done one huge lap

I waited for the waves to drag me west
But I realized I'd have to do the rest
I'm the only one who can make the trek
With each stroke I came closer to
My destiny, it's gonna be something new
This is when I pull my life stage soundcheck

There was that sweet, sweet whine of a guitar wailing out to the heavens, making hopeful banter out to the back of the house. She took a few steps back and continued to strum; she focused on the audience before her, allowing their guitarist to have his moment in the sun. She couldn't help but let a smile spread across her lips. She took in the room full of people and the stage that felt suddenly huge. Sounds weren't tight and couldn't be nailed down to a pinpoint. They bounced off the walls and the other instruments and the other people.

Finally, all four of them took their final strums, their final plucks, their final beats, and it was over so quickly it felt like it had never even happened in the first place. The lights dimmed down a little bit and what she saw was Summer standing right up at the front, of course, cheering on Jas. Next to her though, was Josie. Carla's disappearing act had done one thing she'd ever expected it to - connect her to her sister for the first time in their lives.

Carla blocked out the noise of the crowd and the announcements from the host. She ran back stage and circled around to the front, sneaking behind Josie. Her sister turned and she embraced her in the biggest hug she could.

"I thought the last time I'd see you would be at Sunday dinner."

"I knew you were performing tonight, I got the info from Summer."

"Thanks, I can't believe you came here."

"Of course, Carl."

She looked at her big sister; amazed they'd reached a place together only just as she was leaving. "Josie?"

"Yeah?"

"I think I'm gonna miss you."

"Come here," she pulled her back into another hug, "I'm really gonna miss you too."

"Guys," Summer piped in. "No one is dying here. She's moving to California, not Mars."

"You want a ride home?" Josie asked.

"You don't wanna stay and see how you guys did?"

"No," Carla said, "that wasn't the point. I'll see you and Jas tomorrow though, right?"

"Tomorrow afternoon. You got it."

"Okay, buh-bye."

And with that, Carla and Josie walked out together and took a long car ride home, spending their last seconds together in silence. That silence was perfectly fine.

Carla slept on a rock hard floor that night, having sold off her mattress. Shockingly, hardwood didn't make for a comfortable surface. She rolled up a couple shirts and rested her head on them, lying on her back. She could still see the one last photo that remained on her wall and in less than twenty-four hours two dimensions would become three and she would be able to reach out and touch it all.

Applying the word sleep to that night was also being a bit gratuitous. She wanted to blame it on the unfortunate surface, but there was a long flight ahead of her, followed by an unspecified length of uncertainty. The sun finally crept in, relieving her of the duty of masquerading under the guise of sleep, and she sat up on her butt, leaning against the wall. It wasn't really all that more comfortable, but it was at least better. She picked up the rolled up ball of shirts and shoved them in the duffel that Josie had given her. Apparently, it was Nick's, but she insisted he would be grounded and not traveling for quite some time. By noon she had walked through her apartment several times, cleaned, and cleaned again. Her landlord came by to collect her keys and check through the space, though she wasn't even sure why. She had lived there so long without incident, that it would unbelievable to be accused of any damage or wrong doing, particularly where the steps leading into the building were a whole mess of their own.

"So, you find a new tenant?" she'd asked.

"Naw, not yet, I'm renovating it first."

"Oh figures, just wait for me to leave and then fix it up."

"You've been on rent control for years, what the hell, am I fixing it up for that? Naw, This baby's gonna get a new bathroom, a real size fridge, and poof! I think I can get fifteen, sixteen hundred a month."

"Jesus."

"Yep, it's still a shame you're leaving, I never heard a peep out of you. Good luck with whatever you do."

"Thanks," she had said, "I'll need it."

Now, she sat on the floor with only Nick's duffel, her backpack, and a guitar. She set her phone down and let it serenade her for a couple more hours, checking off in her mind that she had done everything she'd needed to and then double-checked again.

Finally, as it was once again dark out, Summer and Jas had arrived and buzzed her to come down. She looped her backpack through the armholes and assigned each hand to one remaining possession. She opened the door and stood there, trying to look at her little apartment that didn't seem so little anymore, now that what few possessions she'd had were removed from it.

The lights were turned out and she stepped into

the hallway, closing the door behind her. The lock clicked into place and she knew that it was over. She tried jiggling the doorknob, but she was officially locked out. The only option left was to move on.

Downstairs, she found Summer and Jas, both leaning against the car. Jas took the duffel, "So are you ready?"

Carla looked at both of them, "Not really, no."

"Well, you're shit outta luck then."

Jas took her guitar next and threw that in the truck as well. He slammed it shut. "Come on, let's go."

"Hugs first," Summer demanded. "It's impossible to hug at the airport."

"You make good points." Carla exchanged what felt like the millionth hug in the last few days. When they were done, everyone wordlessly assumed their positions in the truck.

"Can I get a song?" Carla requested.

"Always," Summer replied.

The sounds of a piano floated in to the back seat accompanied by a tenor casually singing about pre-flight bags being packed.

"Oh, Elton John? Haha, very funny."

"I can't resist."

Elton would do just perfectly as it turned out though, the swinging summer time infused lilt to his voice as "Rocket Man" shot from Jas' speakers carried them through the back roads of Cambridge and sent them shooting down the tunnel until they emerged at departures.

"So Carla," Jas turned back and looked at her after he pulled over, "is it gonna be a long, long time?"

"Our final moments together, and that's what you go with? I can't even."

"Don't *not even* with me now, dude," Summer mocked.

"Okay, fine, I can't stay mad at you. *I even.*"

"We'll miss you."

"I'll miss you more, I promise."

"Okay, stop being mooshy and get the hell out of my truck."

"Fine, I love you, bye." Carla emerged from the car, retrieved her duffel, backpack, and guitar and walked into the airport for the first time in ten years.

As soon as Carla had sunk into her assigned seat, she lost all recollection of what was going on around her. She plugged her headphones in and hit shuffle, a tribute to her days going forward. Simian's "La Breeze" greeted her first and she forced herself to accept the music given to her, to say goodbye to this song once it was over, and the fact that she wouldn't know what would happen once the final seconds of this song were over.

The plane had taken off; the best part of a flight where every bit of human and machine rumbled, accurately matching the feelings in her stomach. Finally, they were up in the air with hours of nothing before her. They climbed higher and higher; Carla's head filled with air and floated above her a few feet, or so it seemed. Between the exhaustion of the day and her racing mind that night, as soon as they were cleared to, she flopped the tray table in front of her open. She took off her sweater and balled it on top of the tray. Finally, she was able to sleep.

She slept through that entire night on the plane. When they landed, the morning was a dusky looking blue. The sky confused Carla, but she realized that dawn by the ocean here wasn't immediately met with sun. As they came in closer to El Segundo, Carla ripped out her earbuds and peered over her snoring neighbor. Light illuminated the sky, being interrupted only by the scant clouds. The neighborhoods sprawled below her, reaching out to the horizon, but it was the blue black that remained in the distance over the sea that was most intriguing.

The plane touched down, and several more cramped moments later, she was liberated from her pressurized metal cage. Wandering in a daze, she made her way to baggage claim and found her luggage, amazingly enough, intact. Outside, there was a cabstand; she meandered over to it.

A gruff, haggard gentleman whose nametag was emblazoned with *Sid* looked up at her. "Where you headed?"

"That's the question."

"What?"

As Sid most likely wasn't looking to for a philosophical debate, but a literal location, Carla opened her mouth and went with the first thing that popped out of it. "Lo Porto."

"Alright then."

She followed Sid to a cab and clumsily lumbered into it. The driver took off, speeding down exit ramps out of the airport and on to palm tree lined multi-lane streets. It was beautiful and hideous at the same time.

Towards Manhattan Beach they drove. Lo Porto was where her photo had been taken. Arlo lived in some place called WeHo. She wasn't sure where that even was in relation to the beach, but she assumed no one in their right mind would be awake at five thirty in the morning on a Saturday, so returning to the scene of the crime felt safest.

The cab driver pulled over to the side of the street next to The Strand and she grabbed all her possessions and fell out with about the grace with which she'd clambered in.

Straightening up, she plugged her earbuds back in and kicked her shoes off, shoving them into her backpack. She set her song to "Itchin' on a Photograph" and marched her guitar and duffel through the sands, trying to march to the beat of the handclaps in the song. As the lead singer took up his vocals at the beginning of the song she found a spot she could mark as her own and dropped her belongings on either side of her.

The chorus clunked on and the sound brought everything into color, the blue started melting into pink and a female voice came into play in her ears. She wondered if the lead singer's blood vessels ever threatened to pop. The waves crashed close to her and off in the distance, surfers popped up and down, depending on their ability to balance and slide through the waves.

With the sun at her back and the universe before her starting to glow with warmer colors, the final lyrics were delivered with a fiery gusto and forceful holler, which culminated in guitar that sang in falsetto. With the final strums of electrical guitar, Carla sat up straight and unlocked her guitar case. As the hand claps faded out and the song ended, she flipped open the lid. She was ready to start making her own music.